I0671383

BOOKS BY SKOOT LARSON

The Lars Lindstrom Zen Jazz Mystery series

The No News is Bad News Blues

The Real Gone Horn Gone Blues

The Dig You Later Alligator Blues

The On the Road Again Blues

The Dave Holman "Texas" Mystery series

The Texas Detective

The Pachyderm Predicament

Political Humor

Apollo Issue, a Humorous Look at Healthcare

The Palestine Solution

The Pachyderm Predicament

a Dave Holman Mystery

Skoot Larson

Skoot's
Jazz
Books

© 2016 by Skoot Larson

All rights reserved. No part of this book may be reproduced, stored in a retrieval system or transmitted in any form or by any means without the prior written permission of the publisher, except by a reviewer who may quote brief passages in a review to be printed in a newspaper, magazine, journal or literary website.

First printing

All characters in this book are fictitious, and any resemblance to real persons, living or dead, is coincidental

ISBN: 978-0-578-17655-0

Published by Skoot's Jazz Books

Rockport, Texas

For the members of the Rockport Writer's Group, whose enthusiastic response to the original idea of Dave Holman, The Texas Detective, encouraged me to soldier on and create a novel from that short story. Thanks for your encouragement! It is something all of us creative people need constantly! And, again, thanks to my editor, Theresa Feeser, for her patience and attention to detail. It wouldn't be possible without you.

CHAPTER ONE

"Why don't you take Sammi for a walk?" she told me. "You know Sammi loves the beach!"

"Okay," I said, planning to take a walk on Rockport Beach anyway.

Having grown up on the California coast near Los Angeles, Rockport Beach wasn't that impressive to me. It was a south facing stretch of Aransas Bay that, some thirty years previous, had been filled in and covered with imported sand. It stretched roughly a mile from the yacht harbor jetty to the county fishing pier and the strip of sand was around 75-feet wide, with small thatched straw umbrellas the locals called Palapas planted every few yards to provide shade from the strong Texas sun. Animals were only permitted on the easternmost edge of Rockport Beach, across the road from our landmark giant aluminum and fiberglass statue of a blue crab. The Chamber of Commerce advertised it as the largest blue crab in the world. I was careful to steer Sammi well onto the animal friendly piece of beach.

And now here I stand, surrounded by three Rockport policemen, a pair of shotgun toting ladies from Aransas County Animal Control and the harbormaster for the Aransas County Navigation District.

Sammi is a small baby elephant, somewhere around half a ton. My partner, Yolanda, had rescued Sammi from a run-down roadside zoo just outside Houston a few days earlier. Yolanda ran a non-profit charity called the Rockport Elephant Rescue. When I first met Yolanda, I assumed her elephant rescue was a scam. How many elephants are there to save in Texas?

But Yolanda proved to be legitimate. She collected a lot of donations, but she *did* rescue elephants, what elephants there were in Texas in need of rescue.

And me? I'm a private detective. The only private detective in Aransas County for whatever that's worth. The money isn't great.... Actually, the remuneration sucks, but living on an affordable semi-tropical beach full of colorful birds, gentle deer and beautiful foliage made it worth the sacrifice.

Be that as it may, here I was on Rockport Beach surrounded by public officials. I had taken our rescued baby elephant, Sammi, for a walk as requested. I had parked our truck on the east end of the beach, where 'pets' were permitted and ankled out to the edge of Aransas Bay. So far, so good.

Sammi became very excited when she saw the water. She ran into the subdued surf, such as it is on Rockport Beach.

Who could have known there would be a very staid and sheltered family of tourists from Oklahoma sitting on canvas chairs along the water's edge? Sammi greeted them with a loud, bombastic trumpet, then sprayed a trunk full of salt water over their little tribe, a move that struck terror into their hearts, for some reason.

A handful of small children in another nearby group of vacationers laughed at the Oklahoma party, squealing with joy as Sammi rolled her body in the shallow water and waved her fat little legs in the air.

Sammi continued her romp out into the waters of the Gulf of

Mexico from there, but the Oklahoma tourists remained shore-bound and cowering in terror. Cell phone came out and 911 calls were made.

The first responders were friends, who had a hard time suppressing laughter as they logged the family's complaint. They were drinking buddies of Yolanda's and mine, and were always quick to acknowledge that I often helped our local gendarmerie with crime in our town, sharing my 'big city' experience. Before coming to Texas, I had been a detective second grade in Los Angeles. In spite of our good working relationship, the locals needed to do their job to insure the well-being of tourists in our beachside community. Tourism is Rockport's number one industry.

Animal control was next on the scene. While the stocky gray-haired senior lady in uniform wanted to shoot Sammi without further question, cooler heads prevailed, reminding her that there *was* an elephant rescue in town that could be called. I tried to tell the woman that *I* was part of the elephant rescue over the hoots and guffaws of the local cops.

In the end, the woman called Yolanda, my partner, who arrived quickly, dressed in her yellow sari with the red dot on her forehead.

"Can't I trust you to do anything?" she asked me for openers in a put-on Indian sing-song accent. "You were just supposed to take our dog, Spot, for a short walk and look what happens!" Yolanda was having a difficult time suppressing laughter of her own and her phony mode of speech was faltering with her mirth.

By now, the cops, the harbormaster and the animal control ladies were doubled over with laughter of their own. The Oklahoma tourists, however, didn't seem to get the joke. They looked around as if a flying saucer had just carried them away to some distant outer world.

The Rockport Police Sergeant in charge made a big show of writing me a ticket, explaining between fits of giggling that "Spot" was not a dog and I had no right to frighten the tourists. This gave the Okies some minor satisfaction although their mumbling among themselves indicated that they would be headed for Port Aransas or Corpus Christi as quickly as they could get their bags packed.

In the parking area, as he helped us nudge Sammi up the ramp into our rented stake truck, the sergeant turned away from the beach, tore up the citation and tossed it over our heads like ticker-tape parade confetti. "I hope you've learned something here, Holman," he chuckled, patting Sammi's rump as she cleared the tailgate. "And if not, we'll explain it to you up at Rusty's later to-night. And I'll buy the first round of drinks! Only fitting for the entertaining afternoon you've provided."

He thought for a minute, then added, "And I think a few more of the guys on the force will be happy to spring for a few beers too! This afternoon was a classic! Only in Rockport!" he laughed.

CHAPTER TWO

After we'd brought Sammi back to her pen behind the feed and fence store where Yolanda and I shared an office, unloaded our charge into her shelter and made sure she had food and water, Yolanda told me I'd had a visitor earlier in the afternoon.

My visitor had been a Hispanic lady who had seemed very distraught. She had gotten my name from Brenda, a waitress at Rusty's Tropical Café and Bar, who had given me a glowing recommendation, but the lady wouldn't say any more. She didn't want to leave a name, address or number. She said she would call back when she could, but sounded desperate to talk to someone immediately. Yolanda said the woman had been close to tears, when she had learned I wasn't in the office.

Yolanda had tried to comfort her and keep her waiting for me, but the woman's eyes had been crazy, darting around our small office without finding a place to rest.

She had mentioned that, as she was in Texas illegally from Mexico, she was terrified that she might be sent back to Merida before her situation could be resolved. She offered no more information and Yolanda had to let her go when the call came in from Animal Control about Sammi on the beach.

Later that evening, when we joined our cop buddies at Rusty's, I tried to question the night wait staff about anyone who might be seeking my services, but no one could give me a clue.

Yolanda and I normally came into Rusty's for Happy Hour in the afternoon. The day bartender, Cat, was the person we knew best after Rusty himself.

Harley, the night bar tender couldn't recall anyone asking about my services, but said she would check around with Brenda and the waitresses she knew on the other shifts and get back to me. I offered a business card but she laughed and said, "Rusty knows where to find you."

The Rockport cops were in a fun mood. One patrolman pulled his pants pockets out like ears and threatened to unzip his pants to give us his impression of Sammi walking on the beach. His sergeant stopped him, but just barely as he was laughing almost too hard to control himself.

The local law enforcement bought us two or three rounds of beers and Yolanda and I bought them all shots of Jameson's Irish whisky to compliment the suds. Around ten in the evening, the animal control ladies walked through the door to join the party. They were dressed in mufti, but easily recognizable. The senior officer apologized to Yolanda for her threat to shoot Sammi, saying she had been caught up in the heat of the moment and that she had always wanted to shoot *something*, especially now that it was legal for folks to 'open carry' weapons in Texas. She had been armed by the county, but dealt mostly with cats, dogs, squirrels and raccoons. There were few animals for her to control that truly proved a threat beyond a small net, and she became carried away at the thought of a large wild creature she could subdue.

Yolanda told her it was okay, but I could see in her eyes that it wasn't. My Indian lady's brain was busy calculating how to get back at this redneck member of officialdom.

We were able to excuse ourselves just before midnight. The sergeant was chatting up a divorced lady visiting from Kansas and one of the younger cops was busy being seduced by the younger animal control officer, a typical Texas Thursday night. We payed our tab and snuck out without formal goodbyes.

Back in our small apartment behind the office we shared between my detective agency and Yolanda's elephant rescue, we retired and quickly fell into a sound sleep. The day had taken its toll and the beer and whiskey had only added to the day's exhausting effects.

I was dreaming that I was back in Los Angeles, driving my unmarked cruiser down West Adams Boulevard where a local gang had threatened to kill one police officer a day until a local gang leader was released. That gang peddled meth to the local middle schools, so any leniency had been deemed out of the question.

In my dream state, a teenager in black clothes and backward Raider's cap suddenly popped up in front of my windshield. He held something out in front of him, and I heard a series of rapid staccato thumps, like the sound of a silenced gun.

I must have screamed in my sleep. I awoke to Yolanda rocking me in her arms.

"It's alright, Dave," she crooned. "You're okay, just calm down!"

My eyes flew open, but the popping of bullets continued. "Wha's that?" I whispered sleepily.

"Someone's at the door, out in the office," Yolanda cooed reassuringly. "If you're okay, I'll go see who it is. Are you okay now?"

I nodded lamely and my lady rose from our bed and pulled a long tee-shirt over her head. She went through the kitchen and the outer door to see who might be calling at three in the morning. I pulled on my cargo shorts and a parrot covered Hawaiian shirt to await my summons.

I heard subdued voices from the outer office, then Yolanda returned to inform me that my mysterious Hispanic client had returned.

"At three in the flippin' morning?" I asked rhetorically, but I received no answer, so I followed my partner into the main office to confront my mystery client.

CHAPTER THREE

The woman's name was Lupe Martinez and she was in an extremely agitated state. Her 15-year-old daughter, Chandra, had been snatched right in front of her friends four days earlier on her way home from Rockport Fulton High School. Chandra's friends said she had been grabbed and dragged into a beat-up gray van, the kind with no windows, often used to make commercial deliveries. None of her friends could quite agree on a description of the man who grabbed Chandra, but they were all sure he was wearing low-slung baggie blue jeans and that he had longish blond hair. One girl had mentioned cowboy boots and another claimed the man had something tattooed on his arm, but none of the others could confirm seeing either a tattoo or boots. No one had thought to look at the van's license plate.

Chandra had been taken very close to her small rented home on North Kossuth Street. Neighbors, those who would speak to Lupe, couldn't remember seeing anything. Some of Lupe's neighbors, she said, were what people call 'rednecks' that resented a Mexican single mother living in the neighborhood. When she had tried to get their help, they told her, "Serve's you right for comin' to *our* country illegally," and "Why don't you go back where you came from."

"I flagged down a policeman near our street that evening," she told me. "He is the one that told me that if I asked for help, I would be deported. He said America helps its own and that there are too many of us wetbacks here in Texas."

"That's a bunch of bull! Did you get his name? Or his badge number?"

"No," she replied. "I'm afraid I just burst into tears. He laughed at me, got into his patrol truck and drove away."

"Lupe," I tried to assure her, "this man is *not* typical of our Rockport police force. If we can find out who he is, he will be reprimanded and possibly fired. The police can and will help you. I can talk to them for you...."

"No, I don't trust the police! If you want to have them help, you can talk to them, but I want to hire *you*, Mr. Holman. I will trust you to find my daughter!"

"Lupe, the police can bring in the FBI after 24-hours. Kidnapping is a federal offense and it will be dealt with seriously, whether you are a citizen or not!"

"You will deal with this seriously," she told me, nodding her head with a stern face. "I've heard many good things about you. Everyone says that if anyone can find Chandra, it is you."

"I don't come cheap," I told her. "I require a fee of $75.00 an hour plus expenses. I can give you a discount, but it still adds up quickly. The police are already paid to help and won't cost you anything."

"And if there are more policemen like the man I spoke to," she countered, "I will get just what I pay for, *nada*, nothing!"

Yolanda was staring hard at me. Her eyes were telling me I should do what I can for this poor woman.

"Do you have a photograph of Chandra?" I asked.

Lupe withdrew a handful of pictures from her coat pocket and spread them on my desk like a dealer showing a winning hand. I caught a quick breath.

Chandra Martinez did *not* look fifteen. She looked well over twenty-one, and built, as they used to say, like a brick silo! This girl would get a double-take from the ghost of Hugh Hefner! In the first photo, she stood in front of the Rockport Beach Pavilion wearing a yellow polka-dot bikini and high heeled sandals. She had long auburn hair and longer legs with breasts that rich young girls paid plastic surgeons more for than some people paid for their homes.

Other photos included a school portrait of a smile most men would die for, a candid of her with girlfriends at a high school football game, and one of her with a smiling Rockport football hero after a local game.

Yolanda gave me a dirty look to say I was staring at the pictures for too long. I shuffled them back into a short deck, separating the school portrait to the side to enlarge and show around for my investigation. I gave the rest of the pile back to Lupe.

"There's still the matter of my fee," I told her without much heart in it. "I'll need a retainer of at least a thousand dollars."

Lupe brought out a thick wad of bills from another coat pocket and peeled off ten pictures of Ben Franklin. "I've been saving in hopes that Chandra will go to college," she offered with a resigned look. "If I can't get my daughter back, this will be wasted anyway."

"This money…" I began.

"Since I came to America twelve years ago," she explained, "I have worked always at least two jobs. I clean houses, I do laundry and I waitress so that Chandra will have the good life I never could have. In the past few years, waitressing has brought me good tips, so I have more time to spend with my daughter. And to go to night school classes myself as well! I still take in some washing, but…"

Yolanda's hip swung out to nudge me. "Mr. Holman will find your daughter," she said, looking down at me with positive eyes. "If you can give me all your information, like phone numbers at home and at work…"

"Oh please," Lupe said, "must you call me at work?"

"Only in an emergency," I assured her.

Yolanda dismissed me with a look. "Mr. Holman will be starting a case file," she said, her eyes telling me that I could go back to bed. "I'll take all your information and put it into our computer. We will be in touch with you by late tomorrow."

I pushed my chair back from the desk, stood and made my exit.

CHAPTER FOUR

In spite of my night of interrupted sleep, I was up at first light. Yolanda already had strong coffee brewing and Nan bread heating in the oven. I wrapped a handful of fresh local shrimp in the warm Indian bread for a quick breakfast, then headed out Market Street toward our civic center.

At the front desk of the police station I asked if Lola Sanchez was in yet. Lola was plainclothes, and in my estimation, one of the smartest detectives I'd ever met. I often wondered why she hadn't moved to a bigger department like Houston, Dallas or even Corpus Christi, but Lola was a single mother with a son and a daughter in local schools. The word was she believed a bigger city with more opportunities for advancement in law enforcement would also mean more exposure to crime for her children. She felt her kids would have a safer and happier life in a small tight-knit beach community like Rockport.

Lola was at her desk doing paperwork, the bane of all public officials, especially crime fighters. I stood quietly in front of her, waiting for her to notice I was there rather than break her train of thought. After a minute, Lola looked up.

"You come in to confess that you drove home from Rusty's drunk again?" she smiled. "'Cause if you did, it isn't any news, you *always* drive home from Rusty's drunk. Hell, Holman, I don't think you'd be able to find your way if you were sober!"

"The lady of a thousand laughs," I replied, projecting my voice out to an imaginary audience behind the woman's desk.

"Okay, Holman, too early for a lot of laughs. What can I do for you?"

I gestured to her visitor chair and Lola nodded for me to sit. "I've got a client that tells me her teenage daughter has been kidnapped," I told her with my most serious face.

"Custody problems with a divorced father?"

"Not that easy, Lo, this girl was grabbed off the street by a guy in a gray van. The father is probably miles away in Mexico and may not even know he has a daughter."

"But you can't prove it wasn't the father?"

"I never thought to ask," I apologized, "but I really don't think this thing is domestic. The girl's friends who witnessed the snatch said it was a young guy with baggy jeans and long blond hair. My first thought was that we've been hearing rumors of a human trafficking ring in south Texas."

"That's a pretty big leap, Holman. From a girl grabbed off the street to a trafficking ring…"

"The girl's mother is illegal. Most of the young ladies who have disappeared have been immigrants. By the way, one of your compadres here in Rockport's finest told the girl's mother to be quiet, that she'd be deported if she came to the police."

"You know that's a load of hooey, Dave! We are here to protect everyone who lives in Rockport regardless of…"

"I know, I know. That's what I told the woman, but she's terrified that she might be deported without getting her daughter back."

"I'll personally look into who in the department might have said something like that and I'll personally kick him in the nuts! So now can you give me some details on this thing so I can get a case started here?"

I brought Chandra's picture out of my pocket and laid it on Lola's blotter. "Her name is Chandra Martinez," I told her. "The mother, Lupe Martinez rents a home at 932 North Kossuth Street. The girl was grabbed just around the corner on Sabinal. She was coming home from school with friends."

"And how long ago?"

"Had to be last Tuesday," I confessed.

"Jesus, Holman. You sure took your time coming to me!"

"Hey, the mother only contacted my office yesterday. And when she came in to the shop, I was on the beach surrounded by all your colleagues who were trying to bust me for walking a rogue elephant. I didn't get to talk to the lady until around three this morning!"

"I heard you closed Rusty's with some of the guys from patrol last night. Maybe if you'd been in your office paying attention to duty...."

"Lola, the woman was terrified she might be deported. She waited until early morning to come to the office because...."

The lady detective laughed at me. "Just pulling your chain, Holman, I know how these things work. Now how soon can you get this woman in here to file a complaint?"

"That's part of the problem," I told her. "She doesn't trust the police. She wants me to take care of the whole enchilada myself. She won't talk to you except through me."

"Holman, why is everything you bring to us so complicated?"

CHAPTER FIVE

Yolanda managed to get Lupe into our office at 10:30 the next morning, just before she was scheduled to go to her place of work. I introduced Lola simply as someone that was helping me. Her position with the Rockport Police could be mentioned later after the lady had earned Lupe's trust.

Lupe talked with parental pride about her daughter, the girl's excellent grades in school and how she seemed to be a model teenager. We also got her to share the names of the friends who had witnessed the abduction on Sabinal Street. When Lola told her that those friends would need to be questioned about that afternoon, Lupe gave me a frightened look.

"But I've told Mr. Holman everything they told me," she replied meekly. "I don't want to put pressure on Chandra's friends."

"It's important that we interview each of them," Lola told her. "It won't have to be at police headquarters, I can speak to them here in Mr. Holman's office or…"

"Police headquarters?" Lupe gasped. "I don't want… I can't…. So are you the police?"

"I'm Detective Lola Sanchez with the Rockport Police, yes. There is only so much Mr. Holman can do for you. With our resources he will have a much better chance of finding Chandra. That is what you want, isn't it?"

Lupe's terrified eyes moved rapidly between Lola and myself. "But Mr. Holman, I hired you so we wouldn't have to involve the police! I don't like the police! I think you have betrayed me!" Her chair scraped back as she started to stand up.

At that moment Yolanda entered from the door to our apartment just off the office. She placed a hand on Lupe's shoulder and spoke soothingly to her. "Please sit back down, Ms. Martinez. Mr. Holman knows what he's doing. Detective Sanchez and several other Rockport officers are good friends of ours. I trust them, and I know you can trust them as well. It will be much easier for us to return your daughter to you using the resources our friends in the police can share with us."

Yolanda leaned over sideways and gave Lupe a reassuring hug. Lupe Martinez relaxed visibly after a few seconds.

"I can really trust them?" she asked me, "I won't be sent back to Mexico for causing America trouble?"

Lola reached across the table, laying her hand on Lupe's wrist. "Nobody wants to send you to Mexico. You are a hard working member of our community. We respect that and we want to help you. That's our job! With Detective Holman's help, we will do our best to reunite you and your daughter. But we will have to question people along the way, like your daughter's friends and maybe even some of your neighbors… and I give you my word, I won't be taking any shit, pardon my French, off any of your neighbors who might not have the proper respect for you. My job is to serve and protect and that is what I do every day!"

CHAPTER SIX

ack at police headquarters, Lola had copies made of Chandra's photograph, passing them out to all the detectives and patrol division officers with a BOLO order. She explained that the girl was missing and assumed to be the victim of foul play. She then asked the other detectives on shift to make calls to locate Chandra's friends and to get their parents to agree to bring them to the station after school to be interviewed. We decided it would be best if I was present for the questioning of these girls so I could make a complete report to my client about what we found.

"Are we ready to call in the FBI yet?" I asked Lola while we waited.

"You know the drill, Holman. It's the same here as it is in California. We get twenty-four hours to try and find the girl ourselves before the feds can be involved."

"But it's already been over seventy-two hours since…"

"Yeah, well it's only been about seven hours by my clock. Seven hours since anything was reported to us. Come on, Dave, you know how these things work!"

"I know that every hour that passes reduces our chances of ever finding Chandra Martinez. If it is a gang of white slavers, she may already be out of the country, on her way to Saudi Arabia or Shanghai."

The lady detective gave me a frustrated look. "Dave, I do things by the book. That's how it has to be. If I called the feds right now and laid it all out for them, they'd still tell me we don't have enough to prove kidnapping. By tomorrow morning, after I talk to the girl's friends and some other people, I should have enough to convince the feebs we have something they need to look into. Just be patient!"

Lola looked down at her notes but I continued to stare at her. When she brought her eyes back to mine, she told me, "Why don't you go home for awhile, Dave. There isn't anything you can do here. Maybe you'll think of something back in your own office. Just keep your mind open and your head clear...

"And don't just drive up to Rusty's for a beer or three! I need you in my office and sober when we get these girls in here to interview."

Back at my own digs, I called our newly re-elected state senator, Burt Jenkins. The senator, who was a former client, owed me a favor or two for exposing his brother-in-law, a corrupt minister who had been using Jenkins and his office for illegal purposes.

"I'm seriously concerned," Jenkins told me, "for both the mother and the daughter, even though if the mother isn't here legally, she can't vote for me. On the other hand, Holman, you know as well as I do that kidnapping is a federal offense. The Rockport Police, the Aransas County Sheriff, they're very good and they will do all they can for this woman along with the FBI."

"Thanks anyway, Senator."

"Hey, Dave, you know I'd help if there was something I could do. I'm grateful to you for changing my life and for helping me keep my office. And I like you, Dave, I really do! Please keep me up to speed on this thing, okay?"

I told him I would stay in touch and we rang off, then I sat for awhile drumming my fingers on the desk top. I wanted a drink, I wanted one badly, and I knew there was a bottle of cheap blended scotch within easy reach in my desk drawer.

Finally, Yolanda came in to distract me. "Budhan, Darpaknu and Payush will be taking Sammi to the elephant refuge in Tennessee tomorrow," she told me. "I'm going to miss that baby. She's probably the youngest elephant I've ever helped."

Budhan and the others were part time volunteer helpers in Yolanda's business, the Rockport Elephant Rescue. They came whenever Yolanda called and they were an excellent team; very knowledgeable about the care of pachyderms.

As I said, when I first met Yolanda, I'd assumed the elephant rescue was some kind of scam, but I was quickly proved wrong when the call came that there was an abused animal out by Lake Corpus Christi and Yolanda's Uncle Jishnu flew down from New York to round up their team and answer the call.

"Sammi sure made a hit at the beach," I chuckled. "I'll never forget the look on the faces of those Okies."

Yolanda's eyes misted over briefly. "Oh, Dave! I wish I could keep Sammi, she's so sweet!"

"When you get old, you can become an elephant lady," I kidded her. "I think they say cat ladies have at least seventeen cats. You can get an old house on a few acres of land and collect seventeen or more elephants."

Yolanda's eyes dried and she had to choke back a snort of laughter. "Oh God, what a picture! And you'll be there with a big shovel to keep the yard clean?"

"Anything for you, Babe," I told her as I reached for the ring-ing telephone.

CHAPTER SEVEN

Two of Chandra's school friends were on their way to the Rockport cop shop with their parents. Lola told me that a least one set of parents were not happy to be called in. Their daughter, Carmen, loved Chandra and her mother, the parents did not.

"These illegals are taking all our jobs and sucking up the benefits of our overly generous welfare system," Carmen's father told me when I walked in. "We need to build a solid stone wall along our border to keep all these free-loaders out!"

"I appreciate your taking off from work to bring your daughter here," I told him.

His wife quickly jumped in. "My husband hasn't been able to find work for years," she snarled. "These damn *Meskins* take all the good jobs 'cause they work so cheap!"

"And your husband's profession?" I asked.

"I always wanted to design cars for the big auto makers," he told me. "I got some great ideas for high power, high performance race cars."

"And your educational background for this? Did you study engineering?"

"My husband never got the chance," the wife cut in again. "Our son, Austin come along when we was juniors in high school. Trevor had to go to work bailin' hay for his daddy so we could afford to get married. Then a year and a half later, Carmen was born.

Trevor's daddy sold his ranch shortly after that and Trevor hasn't been able to get a job since. We're just lucky that his daddy gave us the double-wide we live in free-and-clear before he passed."

"So you live on county assistance?" I asked.

"And food stamps, when we can get them," the father added.

"And you're complaining about a woman who works two jobs to support herself and her daughter and doesn't ask for any help?"

"Don't go there, Holman," Lola cut in. "It isn't important. What is critical right now is what Carmen can tell us about the afternoon that Chandra disappeared."

I sat back under the glare of Trevor and his wife. Obviously, if I was a *good* American I wouldn't be questioning them.

Lola asked if anyone minded her taping the session. "Just so we get everything straight and there are no questions about what was said afterwards." Trevor crossed his arms over his chest and frowned in disapproval, but his wife shook her head in agreement with the idea.

As she pushed the record button Lola recited, "This is Detective Loretta Sanchez interviewing Carmen Roberts. Her parents, Trevor and Alice Roberts, are present along with private detective David Holman. The time is two-fifty-five p.m. Friday, September eighteen.

"Carmen," Detective Sanchez began. "Tell me what happened last Monday afternoon when you were walking home from school? Did you walk straight home?"

"Well," the young lady began with a cautious look in her parent's direction, "we went a little out of our way…"

"Out of your way how?" I queried.

Carmen cast another long look at her parents, then hesitantly began, "Well, we walked down to Laurel and then back up Moline to the dead end, where we cut through some woods…"

"What the hell are you sayin' girl?" the father shouted, coming out of his chair.

Detective Sanchez silenced him with a look and he sat back down. "Why did you go so far out of your way," she asked the girl.

"Well…" Again Carmen was hesitant to speak until Lola gave her a reassuring nod. "There's this boy, Jimmy Jimenez, see. He is just so cute! And he lifts weights out behind his parent's house on Sabinal. I think he knows we walk by there just to watch him, and I think he's showing off for us. He really wants to impress Chandra, but she's already going steady with Bobby Ray, the quarter back on the Rockport Pirates team."

"Okay," Lola continued over the angry stares of the parents. "So you cut through the woods to Sabinal Street, then what happened?"

"When we came out to the street?" Carmen's eyes tracked rapidly between Lola, her parents and myself. "Like, there was this gray van back in the trees on the other side of the road. We didn't pay it no mind 'cause, you know, there's a lot of abandoned cars around there."

"Had you seen this van there before?" I asked.

"I don't think so," Carmen answered, "but then I really only noticed it when it started up and came over to where we were standing. Then this dude jumped out and grabbed Chandra and put a rag or towel or something over her face!"

"Can you describe the man who grabbed Chandra?" Lola asked.

"Well… he was pretty average, I mean he wasn't real tall or anything. He had dirty blond hair hanging to his shoulders, I think, and his arms looked pretty buff."

"Buff?" I asked.

"You know, like muscular? And he had tattoos around his upper arm, like writing, but it didn't look like English writing. It was like weird letters, you know?"

"And how was he dressed," Lola asked.

"He was wearing jeans, but they were really low, like gangsta' low on his legs, you know? And he had on a black tee shirt with a picture of a band on it, but the writing beneath the band's picture was the same weird letters as on his tattoo."

"Russian Cyrillic script?" I asked Lola, but she just shot me a look that said to butt out.

"And did this man say anything?" Lola asked Carmen.

"He said something, but I can't repeat it. It was really vulgar!"

"This is a police investigation, Carmen, you can tell us," Lola prompted.

"I won't have my daughter goin' t'hell for talkin' dirty," the father jumped in.

Detective Sanchez aimed dark eyes at the man that riveted him back into his chair again, and then nodded to Carmen.

"He said Chandra would be a really hot fuck," the girl blushed. "That she would bring in a lot of money for him when they sold her ass."

The parents blushed as well and averted their eyes. Lola got a few more details from Carmen, then spoke into the tiny tape recorder that had been rolling on the table before us. "Three-thirty-nine p.m. Friday, September eighteen, Detective Loretta Sanchez interview with Carmen Roberts and her parents ended. Also present, David Holman, private detective."

CHAPTER EIGHT

When the Roberts family had gone, Lola asked a uniformed officer if he could send in the Burresons. A very tan blond man and woman entered with a statuesque, gangly girl wearing glasses, braces on her teeth and a Corpus Christi "Hooks" baseball cap. The hair falling down the girl's back was straight and strawberry blond. The entire family looked more like California surfers then Texans.

The man walked right up to me with a big smile, extended his hand and introduced himself as Buster Burreson. "And this is my wife, Viv, and our daughter, Amy. I hope we can be of some help. Just terrible, that's what I said when Amy told us what had happened!"

"I'm Dave Holman," I told the man. "I'm a private detective working for Chandra's mother. This is Detective Lola Sanchez of the Rockport Police." I turned and motioned to Detective Sanchez. Rather than offer her hand, Lola motioned to the chairs across from her desk.

"Thank you for bringing your daughter in, Mr. Burreson. You cooperation is much appreciated. I've just got a few questions for Amy. We won't take up too much of your time, I hope."

"That's okay," Burreson answered. "I'm a yacht broker and business is a bit slow right now, so take all the time you need. Oh, and if you know anyone that's in the market for a boat...." He smoothly withdrew a business card from the pocket of his Hawaiian shirt and set it on the desk in front of Detective Sanchez.

Lola looked at the card but didn't pick it up. "Amy, are you comfortable with me turning on a tape recorder while we talk?" she asked. Amy nodded in the affirmative and her parents smiled at each other with pride that their daughter was such a trooper.

Amy's testimony was much like Carmen's before her. Amy hadn't noticed the tattoo or the tee shirt as she'd been too terrified, looking only into the eyes of the man she believed was going to kill them all. She had, however, noticed that the man was wearing cowboy boots as he slung Chandra's limp body into the side door of his van. They were brown boots, quite worn down at the heels. She also remembered that the man had acne scars along his cheeks and forehead.

When Lola Sanchez terminated the interview, Holman felt that they were making some solid progress. Buster Burreson was all smiles, offering to do what he could, even donating money or starting a "Save Chandra Martinez" fund should it become necessary.

One other family had been reached, but had told Detective Sanchez that they didn't want to get involved.

At five-fifteen, Sanchez told me to go home and get a good night's rest. She would be calling the FBI first thing the next morning, Saturday. It was unsure how quickly they would respond, but she wanted me fresh and sober when they did.

Lupe Martinez came to the office after work. Yolanda joined us, offering Lupe one of the plastic lawn chairs we kept across from my desk for clients. I relayed to her what the Burreson and Roberts families had told Detective Sanchez and assured her that, with the help of the police, we were making progress toward finding Chandra.

"Do you work Saturdays?" I asked. Lupe said she did, but she usually went in on a later shift at the diner, starting at four to catch the dinner hour crowd.

"The FBI will be called in tomorrow," I told her. "Sometime in the afternoon they'll probably want to talk to you."

"Is this something I must do?" she asked, her eyes looking fearful.

"They're just people, Lupe, people who have more power and a greater access to criminal information with their data bases and computers. They will speed up the search for Chandra and will help us bring her kidnappers to justice." I reached out and touched her trembling hand. "Tell them as much as you can and they will bring Chandra home to you!"

"But they work for the government. How can we be sure they will not deport me? Many people say I am a criminal just because I am here."

"Deporting victims of crime is *not* their job. Their duty is to bring criminals to justice, plain and simple!" I tried to put as much optimism in my voice as I could, though I knew that the chances of finding Chandra alive were probably some long odds.

"I'll call you tomorrow when Holman knows more about what the FBI men are doing," Yolanda added, giving Lupe Martinez a hug. "If they want to talk to you, I'll arrange a good time for you to meet with them."

CHAPTER NINE

I knew it would be a long and tedious day when I woke up Saturday. Sometime after nine, Lola Sanchez would be contacting the FBI field office, probably the group in San Antonio as they had more clout than the two-man team in Corpus Christi. I decided that I should get a beach walk in early to center myself and prepare for the day ahead.

I got on my bicycle and rode toward Rockport Beach, stopping for breakfast at JJ's Little Bay Café on Highway 35 on my way. I fortified my system with eggs and potatoes in anticipation of what lie ahead, then peddled the remaining two blocks to the water's edge.

Passing our famous giant crab, I decided to go all the way to the fishing pier at the west end and walk the full length of the sand and back. It would give me time to get all my thoughts in order.

Just beyond the halfway point, by the beach pavilion, I heard a loud motor revving close behind me. I turned my head to see a gray van headed directly for my bike. I tried to swerve into the gravel parking area, but the vehicle slammed hard into my rear, throwing me and the bike into the air. For a brief moment I thought about Yolanda's admonition that I should get a bike helmet and wear it.

I came around with an ache in my head and queasy feeling in my stomach, like seasickness. I opened my eyes to a rolling sea and understood my queasiness. My nose itched and I tried to scratch it, only to discover that my hands were tightly tied behind my back. I coughed, and my coughing brought loud, crude laughter from somewhere beyond my field of vision.

I blinked a couple times and a pasty white corpulent face suddenly filled the space before my eyes. It slowly came into focus, dark eyes and red hair, then backed away. Someone jerked me upright by my tied wrists and I could see that the man was much shorter than me. I'm just short of six feet, carrying a few extra pounds around the middle, so I guess you could say I'm a substantial size man. The fireplug before me was dressed in a cheap suit with pant legs too short even for his diminutive legs. Beneath his trouser cuffs were white athletic socks, the type with a blue stripe around the ankle, and he was shod in the type of black lace-up brogues they issue convicts getting out of the joint. His left hand had bloody gauze wrapped around stumps where his first two fingers should have been.

He spoke, and his breath came straight from a graveyard of teeth that had died. "Mr. Holman, how nice to meet you! I'm glad you agreed to come see me!"

"I agreed to come see you?" I asked, all serious.

"Da," he replied.

I looked around me. We were on a run-down shrimp boat that must have been on its last legs. The decks were filthy with fish blood and sea grass. Flanking the man speaking were two men who looked like they might have been homeless in Houston for a year or two. I did a double take on the one to the right of me. He had shoulder-length dirty blond hair, gangsta-style low-slung blue jeans and a black tee shirt with Cyrillic characters surrounding a photo of four guys with guitars. He also had a band of Cyrillic letters circling his left biceps. Our kidnapper!

My, ah, 'host,' firmly grasped my chin between the thumb and forefinger of his good hand and turned my eyes back to his own eyes.

"Mr. Holman, I vant to gif you a vwarnink!"

"You vant to gif me a vwarnink?" I mimicked with a chuckle.

The hand came up so fast I never saw it, but I felt the open palm that slapped my face around hard enough that my teeth cut into my cheek.

"Do not you mock me, my friend!" he shouted, showering my face with his spittle. "I have heard that you are a smart mouth. I do not tolerate a smart mouth! Now listen to me! You and your meddling friends have already cost me greatly"

"Oh really," I replied with a more neutral face.

"Da, really," he replied, eyes boring into mine. "I was a foolish man. I was so taken by this girl Vlad brought to me. I wanted her for my own! These girls will become sex slaves anyway, I told myself, why shouldn't I enjoy her company for a week or so before I pass her along!

"This was not good thinking," he mused. "I was thinking, how do you say? With the small head? So it is not all your fault. But if you had not brought in the police, I might have gotten away with a little pleasure for myself! For this, for taking away my sex toy and for losing my fingers, I hate you, Dave Holman!"

I couldn't help smiling, even if it was risking another hard slap. "So you've sent Chandra on to your bosses?"

"No!" he exploded. "My boss does not want the, how you say, the heat? I am having to let this beautiful specimen go! And as I was just becoming, how you say, acquainted with her! It has broken my heart, but at least I still have my life and my job.

"Which is why I must give you the vwarnink, Dave Holman, to save my own skin, I must insure that you will forget this whole matter! As we speak, this girl is being released free in her neighborhood. She will go home to her mother, and she has promised that she will say nothing. You must tell the police this was all a misunderstanding, that this girl ran away with a boyfriend or something for a few days and that your case is now closed. You must see that all this is forgotten!"

"And if I can't do that?" I asked, sans smile.

"Mr. Holman, accidents happen. Bicycles get hit by cars, as you know. Sometimes the riders, they do not survive. People fall overboard from boats and drown. These things you should know."

I started to laugh and suddenly felt strong hands grabbing my legs and lifting me. Before I could react, I was being tossed over the side of the rusted old tub.

As I flew through the air, I could hear the throttles increasing to a scream. I hit the water, and realized that the rope fastening my hands behind me was some twenty or thirty feet long, coiled on the boat's deck and tied off to the pipe railing across the stern.

The old boat lurched ahead, dragging me behind like some kind of inverted water skier. I planed briefly on my back before the boat's momentum sucked me under. I tried to hold my breath, but my ribs were being buffeted by sharp waves from the vessel's wake.

Just as I was sure I'd breathed my last, someone jerked on the line and pulled me back aboard. My wrists were screaming in pain and I was sure both my shoulders had been dislocated. "Have I made my point?" the old Russian asked. I vomited up my breakfast with a few gallons of seawater in front of him as my reply.

"This is how you repay my hospitality?" he laughed, playfully punching me in the gut again. "You vomit on the deck of my yacht? Well just, how they say in old American movies, 'keep your nose clean, Dave Holman. Or else, the next time you will surely drown for real. Or maybe just lose someone close to you. Your partner is a bit long of tooth for our regular clients, but I'm sure we could make use of her for sex somewhere if you don't cooperate!"

CHAPTER TEN

They cut the rope from my hands and tossed me overboard in Fulton Harbor, just inside the breakwater. I was able to pull myself up on the seawall and walk down Fulton Beach Road to Rusty's.

Rusty met me at the door and told me he didn't want me tracking dirty gulf water into his restaurant. I said it was urgent and he went around and opened the gate to his outdoor patio bar and uncapped a beer for me. When I'd filled him in on what had happened, he went inside for his cell phone and dialed my office for me.

Yolanda promised she would be right over to take me back to my bicycle. She also told me that Detective Sanchez had been calling for the past hour or more, and wanted me in her office ASAP.

Yolanda picked me up outside Rusty's in the old gray VW Thing she drove for her elephant rescue business. We drove down Broadway, along Little Bay to Rockport Beach, where we found my bike in some tall grass on the dunes near the water. The back tire was flat and the rear wheel had been stove in to resemble a crescent moon.

Yolanda tossed the broken cycle into the back of the Thing and shot me a look like I was a small child unable to take care of myself. Eyeing my soaked clothes, she stated the obvious. "You can't meet anyone dressed like that. You'd better grab a shower and let me call ahead that you're on your way to the meeting."

By the time I arrived at police headquarters, Chandra had already knocked on her mother's door and the FBI had begun questioning my credibility.

The two agents were dressed alike in gray slacks, white shirts and heavy blue blazers in spite of ninety degree heat outside. The lead man was taller than me, had dark hair and blue eyes. His partner was the color of strong coffee, his nappy hair so short his head looked like sandpaper.

Lola Sanchez had shown them the testimonies from Chandra's friends, but the federal guys countered that maybe these girls were in conspiracy with their friend, helping her to keep her secret rendezvous with this mysterious boyfriend. Between Detective Sanchez and myself, we finally convinced the two officers that there was reason to believe a crime had been committed, although the two G-men sat across from us with suspicious faces and arms crossed tightly over their buttoned sports coat fronts.

Around two-thirty, a uniform issued in Yolanda along with Chandra and her mother. Extra chairs were brought in for them to sit down.

Chandra had a broken look to her and didn't want to say anything. Lupe was so glad to have her daughter back that she offered little beyond a "thank you all!"

Detective Sanchez threw some questions out to Chandra about what had happened, but Chandra gave robotic answers about her life being private. "If I have such a boyfriend, it's nobody's business," she stated with a brave and defiant stance. Her posture said brave, but I could tell she was seconds away from cracking.

"We will still need your testimony," I told her. "Your friends

Amy and Carmen are guilty of lying to the police and perjury. We will need your statement to send them to prison."

Lola Sanchez started to come out of her chair, but Yolanda grabbed her arm and held her back, shaking her head that Lola should just play along for a minute.

Chandra burst into tears, shaking her head wildly, which sent her weeping water flying over all the assembled folks.

"No!" she screamed. "You can't arrest my friends. They've done nothing but try to help me!"

"They lied to help you. They told lies to the police and the federal government."

The black FBI man started to say something, but this time Lola Sanchez stopped him with a look.

"Chandra," I said in my softest, gentlest voice, "did your friends know you were running off with a boyfriend? And did they lie to protect you?"

The girl threw her head down on the table. "They will kill me. And then they will kill my mother," she wailed.

"Who will kill you?" Lola asked very softly. "Is it the people who kidnapped you?"

Chandra drew a deep, ragged breath. "Yes," she sobbed. "Yes! These men said if I told anyone about them, they would kill me and my mother! Then they said that maybe instead they would just torture us and see that we were sent back to Mexico... as slaves for the drug people!"

The two feds and Lola all let out a deep collective breath.

"Tell us about these men who kidnapped you," Lola Sanchez asked. "They can't hurt you or your mother now. You are under the protection of the police and the FBI. Also Detective Dave Holman, whom your mother has hired to see that no harm comes to you."

The young lady brought her head up and circled her vision around the room, clocking us each in turn. When her young mind was satisfied that we could provide her a certain level of security, she spoke.

"I only vaguely remember someone grabbing me when I was walking home from school with my friends," she told us. "Someone held a chemically smelling handkerchief or something over my face and everything went black. I woke up in a smelly room. Someone had taken my clothes and tied my hands behind me. A short, ugly man with very bad breath kept pawing me all over. His hands on me made me feel sick. He, he... Oh God, I can't even talk about it! It was so gross!" She broke down in sobbing.

Lupe grabbed her daughter protectively and Detective Sanchez halted the interview, saying that Chandra wouldn't be required to say anymore until she had been given counseling.

The feds opened their posture and spoke among themselves, then turned to Lola Sanchez and told her, "I think we may have misjudged Detective Holman and this case. We will be looking into this matter very seriously."

I reminded them of the rumors about a white slaving ring in south Texas. The lead agent, who finally offered a card and introduced himself as Jim Hickok, told me we would be talking again soon. His partner gave me a card as well, introducing himself as Ed Bishop, but he didn't say anything to me.

"We are aware that someone is kidnapping vulnerable young women," Hickok admitted, "children of illegal immigrants and the very poor who are afraid of officialdom. And you understand the difficulties we are faced with in dealing with these folks, who are suspicious of any kind of government."

I told them I understood perfectly, offering my past credentials as a Los Angeles Police officer and my law degree from Cal State Los Angeles for credibility. We agreed to meet again on Monday and discuss how to proceed on the case.

CHAPTER ELEVEN

Sunday was quiet. Lupe stopped by to say how grateful she was to have her daughter back. I offered to return five hundred dollars of her retainer as I hadn't done much more than bring in the police and conduct a few interviews.

"Yolanda told me that Chandra's kidnappers beat you up and almost drowned you!" Lupe replied with wild eyes. "They wrecked your bicycle! I think you have earned all that I gave you, at least enough to buy you a new bicycle."

"It was a very old bicycle," I assured her. "I needed to get a new one anyway."

When Lupe left, I decided to take a walk on Rockport Beach. I desperately needed to center myself and get my head on straight. Yolanda agreed, and promised that when I returned we would have lunch at Rusty's along with a few beers and maybe a shot or two of Jameson's Irish.

I headed out in Yolanda's Thing, her elephant mobile, past the giant blue crab, and parked near the fishing pier and our community's little salt water swimming hole at the west end of the public park. Like most Sundays, Rockport Beach was like a small circus with colorful shade canopies erected all along the water's edge and people in lawn chairs, canvas settees and chaise lounges scattered from the sand out to the shallow off shore sand bars. Children ran along the water's edge collecting hermit crabs in bags and buckets or gathering slurry in pails to construct castles of muddy clay.

I set a path along the sand bars maybe twenty yards out in the bay to avoid the sunbathers and revelers. I watched gulls and herons as they circled overhead and small mullet that swam and occasionally jumped from the dwarfed waves. From time to time, I'd stop and gaze out toward St. Joe's Island where tugs pushed barges along the Intercoastal Waterway.

At one point, I was almost knocked over by a group of young men playing football in the surf. One of the athletes was running backwards in the bay, going out for a long pass and totally oblivious to anyone on the beach apart from his mates. The man missed the ball and fell into me, apologizing politely from the watery seat where he landed, to the amusement of his friends.

In spite of the crowd, I had my meditative rhythm going pretty well by the time I reached the dog park at the east end of the strand. Walking back I started running an analysis of what seemed to be going on. The Corpus Christi paper had hinted in an editorial that organized crime, once locally run on a small scale and later controlled by a sort of godfather hiding behind the veil of a local church, had recently been taken over by some larger, more powerful group.

I knew all about the minister who had tried to take control of drugs, prostitution and other criminal activities in the area as he had been the brother-in-law of my client, Senator Burt Jenkins. I had been afraid when Reverend Clem Gordon was killed that someone else would come along and fill the vacuum he left. Northern Mexico's drug cartels had been a good candidate, but they were busy with internal power struggles all across the north of their nation.

Then Russians started appearing in Corpus, Portland and

even Rockport. Russians had kidnapped Chandra Martinez and then taken me for a short boat trip on the Gulf. The men who had warned me away from looking into Chandra's abduction had mentioned 'clients' that bought girls for sex. They hadn't sounded like they were using these girls in local brothels.

Just as I was thinking again about the idea of international white slavers, I happened to glance toward the Rockport Beach Pavilion passing on my left. And there, following me with his eyes and sticking out like a sway-back mule in a run of thoroughbreds was an out-of-shape figure with a beer gut hanging over a dark blue pair of Speedos. No Cyrillic lettered tee shirt or cowboy boots today, but the long dirty hair to his shoulders and his Cyrillic tattoo were like a bold signature. My young Russian friend from the gray van was clocking my progress down the beach and making no secret of his surveillance; a pretty blatant message that I had better stay in line.

I decided to be bold and take the offensive. I ankled through the shallow water to the sand's edge and then up to my minder, putting my face inches from his own.

"Vlad, isn't it? How special to see you out here. Shall we go somewhere and have a beer?"

The man back-pedaled through the sand and crabgrass, head swinging rapidly side to side, eyes wide and frightened in search of an escape, the hunter suddenly the hunted.

"*Izvinite!* I not know you. A misunderstanding!" He quickened his backward walk, right into a volleyball game where a large Hispanic man pushed him out of the way and to the ground in order to send a serve back over the net.

The blond man in the blue Speedo scrambled to his hands and knees then took off running under the pavilion's elevated deck. I stood and watched his departure. Moments later an engine roared to life and I watched as a beat up gray van flew from the parking area much faster than the posted twenty-mile speed limit.

"You just can't get good help," I told myself as I made my way down the beach to where I'd left Yolanda's car.

CHAPTER TWELVE

Monday morning I walked down to Castaways, our local thrift shop, in hopes of finding a new-used wheel to fix my bike. I carried a couple small wrenches in the pocket of my shorts, just in case.

The volunteer in the sporting goods area told me they didn't stock 'parts,' but did have a couple bicycles outside in their locked compound. I walked out with the man to a courtyard filled with walkers, wheel chairs, children's trikes, a set of metal storage shelves and two rusting bicycles.

The first bike was one of those thin-tired racing affairs with handlebars like a set of sheep's horns, but the one behind it was roughly the same size and shape as my own and had a decent set of gear sprockets on it.

"How much if I just buy the back wheel?" I asked the man.

"You buy the whole bicycle," he told me with a look like I was a thick child. "We don't sell parts, twenty-five dollars for the whole bike."

"Okay, I guess I'll buy the whole thing then."

I went back inside with the man where he explained what I was buying and how much to another volunteer at the registers. I surrendered a fistful of crumpled bills and the first man met me outside the front door with my new cycle. I walked it across the lot and behind some kind of monster truck and looked over my shoulder to see that the clerk had gone back inside. I flipped the bike over, took out my spanners, loosened the rear wheel bolts and pulled the gear assembly out of the rear forks. I tossed the wheel into my nearby car, then carried the rest of the frame to a dumpster at the side of the parking area, where I lifted it into the big trash box.

I had my old bike repaired, oiled and running in plenty of time to take it for a test spin down to the police station and my appointment with the two federal cops. The uniform at the front desk directed me to a spacious conference room in the back of the building. Around an oval-shaped table the Rockport Chief of Police and the Aransas County Sheriff waited along with Lola Sanchez, Jim Hickok and Ed Bishop. Bishop had a leather briefcase open in front of him spilling computer printouts over a laptop that wasn't much bigger then a paperback book.

I pulled a comfortable looking roller chair from the under the lip of the table's north end, opposite the chief and the sheriff. The chief looked at me over the top of his reading glasses. "Holman, I think you know everyone here. Shall we get started? Agent Bishop has gathered some data for us."

I heard light footsteps behind me and turned to find a civilian secretary, a gray haired lady in a business suit and running shoes. The woman carried a tray with cups and a coffee pot. The uniform from the front desk followed her with a large box from Rockport Doughnuts.

The meeting paused as coffee was poured and pastries selected. Hickok put Sweet'N Low in a cup for Bishop, who was still busy arranging his papers, then set a glazed doughnut on a napkin next to it. Bishop mumbled "Thanks," without looking up. The secretary made her exit after leaving another full coffee carafe in the center of the conference table.

Agent Bishop passed handouts around to each of us, took an approving sip of his coffee and then said, "Shall we begin?" The others nodded and began looking over the sheaves of paper.

"As you can see, we do seem to have a Russian presence on the Texas coast lately. We have a group that moved here sometime last year from Coney Island and Brooklyn, New York; most of these guys are just small-time common criminals. The two guys that seem to be running the show tried to muscle their way into New Orleans a while back. The Italians and the red necks made it really rough for them and finally sent them packing. Our most recent information has them settled in Houston, but running their people as far south as Corpus.

In the papers I prepared for you, there's a profile of each of the players that we are aware of including bios and arrest records here in America.

"Sounds like the cold war all over again," I commented. Our local people smiled, but the FBI guys shot me sour looks.

"Just listen, Holman," Hickok told me, "you might learn something."

Bishop shuffled the papers in front of him and began again. "I've got these guys arranged in order of how dangerous we perceive them to be. Our first suspect is Demetri Lubikov, known to his associates as Dee or Daddy Dee. Born in Serbia, he immigrated to Moscow as a young man, took a degree in chemical engineering at Moscow University and was quickly recruited into the KGB. It's rumored that his specialty was extracting information by torturing people using acids, gases and other chemicals.

He dropped out of sight right after the Soviet Union collapsed; he surfaced briefly in Mexico in the early '90s and then later, around 2004, started drawing attention to himself in New Orleans. He has been arrested several times in the Crescent City for extortion and aggravated assault. According to his sheet, he disfigured one prostitute by allegedly throwing acid on her. In Mississippi, he was picked up after he threatened some of the Biloxi casino owners. He told them if they didn't cut him in and allow him the exclusive right to run girls out of their hotels, he would release mustard gas in one of their gaming rooms. As you read on, you'll find numerous other similar arrests.

While the established underworld guys managed to run Daddy Dee out of town, the courts got no convictions because no one ever showed to testify against him.

He ran up a similar list in Houston and Harris County, but same deal. No one has ever testified against him and lesser men in his organization always took the fall for any proven crimes.

Next we have Gorbenko Sergejevič, alias Gorby the Gobbler. Gorby took a degree in Linguistics from the University of Leningrad, rose quickly through the ranks of the Russian Army, ending his career as a General. When the Soviets invaded Afghanistan, Gorby was said to have been in charge of slaughtering any Muslims that opposed Soviet ideology. When Gorby returned to Moscow from Afghanistan, he started organizing the men under his direct command in an effort to pilfer what they could from the Moscow government, including the theft and sale of nuclear weapons and plutonium. It was rumored that he had been arrested in Russia and was to be sent to Siberia, but instead he popped up in New Orleans as Daddy Dee's right hand man. It's thought that Lubikov used his KGB connections to get his friend out of Russia and into America. You can read his arrest record for yourselves later along with the info we have on the lesser guys from the Coney Island mob.

I glanced ahead a few pages and found my kidnapper friend and minder, Vladimir Haliskovich. He was reported to have been enlisted Russian army and a lackey for General Sergejevič. This man was better known for his brawn than his brains. Most his arrests since coming to Texas were for assaults and incidences of vandalism, along with one marijuana possession charge that almost got him deported. His New York rap sheet was about the same but without the pot bust. It made me curious as to how much farther I'd have to read to recognize the middle-management guy who'd lost two fingers and blamed me.

"So we know these men are all seasoned professionals," Hickok was saying. "They are quite capable of organizing and/or driving out the locals. They put little value on human life and have no aversion to killing anyone who gets in their way."

Heads nodded in the affirmative all around the table.

"The sixty-four thousand dollar question," Hickok continued, "is when they made the jump from local racketeering to international white slave trading, if indeed that is what they've done. Did some other group from China or the Arab nations recruit them or did they decide to collaborate with other former Russian intelligence out in the big world and up the ante?"

The discussion continued until late afternoon with no real conclusions drawn beside the fact that we needed to assign some serious manpower to getting answers. The Aransas County Sheriff would contact other sheriff's offices along the coastal bend and closely follow any disappearances and reported possible kidnappings. Our Rockport chief would call a meeting with the leaders of other city police forces in the area, including Port Aransas, Portland and Corpus Christi. I was simply asked to relay anything I might hear to the professionals, let them handle it and not get involved. A tough call for me because I felt like I was already very deeply involved. I wanted to bring Chandra's tormenters to justice, but more than that, I wanted to give Lupe Martinez a sweet taste of revenge on the men that made her feel powerless and degraded her daughter.

CHAPTER THIRTEEN

We had a relaxed Tuesday. I read through all the FBI printouts. In the many pages, I recognized the man with the missing fingers who had brought me to the old shrimp boat to warn me off looking into Chandra's kidnapping. The man was simply known as Chelnikov. It was assumed that this was his last name, but, as he had never been arrested, there was no proof. The pages listed him as an errand boy, a small time player who stayed in the background. One witness claimed he was a driver and pilot for the Russians and he had possibly served as a helicopter pilot for Gorbenko Sergejevič in Afghanistan, but without a full name or some fingerprints it was merely speculation.

After studying all the federal materials on the case, I filled a small hip flask with cheap scotch and took myself for a bike ride and a long walk on the beach. While walking, I mulled over all I had read and learned. I concluded that law enforcement was getting far too complicated. Young girls were disappearing, being hurt, being scarred and led into a hell hole of life hardly worth living. Someone was taking them and using them. We had a long list of pretty good suspects that we *could* arrest to put a stop to all this before more young girls disappeared into the great wasteland of greed and sexual abuse, but so many hoops to jump through, so many boxes to tick off and so many procedures to follow before we could get to the people in question. I decided that it all just made my head hurt. Almost sixteen years in law enforcement, twenty counting my active Coast Guard time in Viet Nam and helping the drug enforcement people, and I still had a hard time making a difference.

I waded after a large bullhead catfish as it swam through the surf and then walked up onto the sand where I turned over hermit crabs pushed onto their backs by the small waves. I finished the last of my scotch and walked unsteadily back to my bicycle in thigh deep water. I thought I glimpsed the gray van tailing me once again, but wrote it off to alcohol and paranoia as I rode my cycle home.

Darpaknu, Budhan and Payush showed up late in the afternoon to take our Sammi to the Hohenwald Tennessee Elephant Preserve. Yolanda prepared a feast for them including curried eggplant with fresh Gulf shrimp, garlic Nan bread and home-made poppadoms from an old family recipe. We washed it down with plenty of Redfish India Pale Ale, after which our rescue friends decided they would put off their departure until after a solid breakfast on Wednesday. The trio bedded down in sleeping bags beside Sammi's pen, taking turns keeping an eye on her although she had been fine for over three weeks without any guardians.

Lola Sanchez called after supper to tell me that the FBI men had gone back to San Antonio around noon, but promised to return with more men and set up a local mission in Corpus Christi from where they could monitor information from all the nearby departments. I told her I was a little pissed off by their attitude that I should just butt out for now. Lola told me that she, at least, valued the work I had done and encouraged me to keep doing what I could, but in low profile so as not to get up the G-men's noses. I had a few more drinks, feeling that I wasn't really appreciated and woke up in my office chair with a blanket tucked around me and sunshine streaming through the office windows. When Yolanda brought me coffee, she also brought stern looks to chastise me for drinking too much again.

CHAPTER FOURTEEN

My stomach was a little rough from the day before. I decided the best thing for it was exercise. After a light breakfast of buttered toast and a beer, I got on my bike and decided I'd cruise the back streets of Rockport, looking for signs of the driver of the gray van that had tried to stalk me. With any luck, he'd be on my tail again and I could brace the man and get some real answers. If nothing else, I'd call Yolanda on my cell and have her drive my old Saab out to run surveillance on where he went after I scared him off.

Yolanda telephoned me around nine, asking me to return home and help her give her rescue boys a good sendoff. After having crisscrossed the neighborhood west of the main 35 Highway for two hours and seeing nothing, I agreed that it was time for a break and returned home. My stomach was settling a bit and my head was clear. I helped coax Sammi up into the truck and accepted hugs from the three young Indian men, then stood with Yolanda and waved as they disappeared down Market and turned left onto Business 35.

Back in the office I told Yolanda what I was doing, that I was looking to catch my minder and turn the surveillance tables on him. My help mate agreed it was a good idea and told me she would be in my car with a wide lens Pentax tailing me, ready to appear wherever she might be summoned to either confirm the man's identity or follow him to his lair.

The young Russian proved to be a late riser. Maybe he'd hit the vodka the night before, or maybe he just liked to sleep in. Whatever the case, he appeared behind my bicycle as I crossed under the 35 Highway on Pearl Street headed for Copano Bay. Turning my head, I could see that Yolanda was close behind the gray van.

I kept peddling along the country road, taking a few turn offs and byways just to be sure I had him hooked. Just past Texas Farm to Market Road 3036, I turned in a semi-circle, blocking the street, and laid my bike down across both lanes. When the man's gray van came screeching to a halt, Yolanda slid sidewise in behind him blocking any escape.

I walked slowly towards the young Russian who once again sent wild eyes searching for an escape. The man backed away from me right into Yolanda's waiting arms. Yolanda threw a set of hand-cuffs onto his left wrist then spun him around to catch his right arm in the bracelets.

Knowing it was bad form, I delivered a quick roundhouse punch to our manacled subject when I reached him. Vlad, if that was his name, fell to his left onto the pavement with a howl, spitting out a tooth along with a slim stream of blood.

"So you've been following me!" I shouted down at his cowering form. "Why are you doing this?"

Both his eyes and lips moved rapidly, but he made no coherent sound. Finally he formed a word. "Please," he screamed, "please!"

"You, my son, kidnapped Chandra Martinez! What do you have to say for yourself?"

"I don't understand," he screamed, "my English is not so good!"

I resisted the temptation to kick him in the crotch, but Yolanda kicked him in the backside, sensing my hesitation. As he flew forward and collapsed by the roadside, I took out my cell and called Lola Sanchez's private number.

Yolanda moved his gray van to the shoulder and we both stood watch over him until the Rockport Police arrived. Uniformed officers read him his Miranda rights as I explained to Detective Sanchez how he had been following me and had, I thought, tried to run me off the road on my bicycle. It was more difficult explaining how my partner just happened to be nearby to rescue me, but Lola Sanchez didn't ask too many questions.

Hickok and Bishop were waiting at the Rockport Police station. Our young suspect was quickly booked for kidnapping, assault and intimidating a witness. At first, he denied any wrongdoing and said he didn't need a lawyer, but in the middle of their first round of questioning, he stopped talking and demanded a telephone call.

His call went to a nameless switchboard somewhere and moments later an attorney from Houston called back, saying he would have someone there within twenty-four hours and no one should try to speak to his client before the man's representative arrived.

Sometime in the night, a Russian Orthodox priest approached the desk at the Aransas County Detention Center wanting to give 'spiritual comfort' to the prisoner. The priest remained for only fifteen or so minutes, then was gone. When jailers came to Vlad's cell with breakfast the next morning, they found that the prisoner had injected himself with an overdose of drugs. No one knew how these drugs could have gotten by the jail's guards.

CHAPTER FIFTEEN

So it was back to square one. Hickok and Bishop didn't say it, but their looks told me that I had screwed up the investigation big time with my meddling.

The gray van was registered to a now defunked Houston plumbing company, no connection to any previous criminal activity although it looked mighty suspicious. The plumbing company's address was non-existent and the company principals were not to be found. Our dead suspect carried no driver's license or other ID. The labels in his clothes were all Eastern European brands.

We had lost our best local lead, but we still had the FBI's long list of Russian gangsters to choose from. I reminded Hickok and Bishop that the man they knew as Chelnikov had been the one, along with young Vlad and another, who had taken me out on the old fishing vessel to warn me off. If Vlad had lived locally, Chelnikov was probably staying in the same location or someplace near to it.

They reminded me that there were hundreds, maybe a thousand old mobile homes sitting on scrub land in the area surrounding Rockport, many fewer apartments, but a large list of vacation rentals that could be hiding our Russian gang. Unless the man made his presence known again, they had nowhere to begin a search. As much as I wanted these men, I really didn't want to continue to act as bait to bring them out.

The cops had a grainy photo of the man they called Chelnikov in the file Bishop had given me. Back at the office, I asked Yolanda to see if she could enhance the photo in her computer and print me a stack of copies. If nothing else, I could go on the offensive and start showing the man's picture all over town. Maybe a checker at the HEB grocery or Walmart would recognize the man and give me some clue about where to find him.

My scotch and gin supply was running just a tad low, so I decided I'd begin my inquiries at The Bottle Brothel, my favorite liquor store just outside Rockport where the female clerks dressed in sexy lingerie and high heels. I could stock up and ask questions at the same time; two birds with one big stone!

Betsy, the proprietor, was seated in her rocker on the porch when I drove up. Betsy couldn't recall seeing the man, but told me it was okay to show the picture to her girls, even leave a copy behind the counter with my number just in case. Betsy and I had a history in that I'd brought a few young people to justice that had tried to rob her store in the past.

I bought a mixed dozen of bottles for the office, some Taaka gin, some Cluny blended scotch and an odd bottle of rum and tequila, along with a couple twelve packs of Redfish IPA. The girls put the boxes in the back of my old Saab and told me not to be a stranger.

I stopped to thank Betsy again and she nodded toward the chair next to hers on the porch. "Sit," she commanded. "This guy you're looking for is some Eastern European type, right?"

"Yeah," I answered. "Russian or Croatian is my guess. Why?"

"Last week some creep in a tee shirt with Russian looking writing on it came in. He pulled a wrench from his pocket and broke a few bottles of good gin and vodka, then told the girls we would need to pay him a few hundred dollars a week and he would protect us, make sure no more of our stock got wasted."

"Geez, Betsy," I showed genuine concern. "So what happened then?"

"The girls hit the button under the counter that sets off a little buzzer under my chair. I walked in and racked a shell into Baby Betsy here." The woman caressed the shotgun she always kept close to her seat on the porch. "Most criminal types know that sound. Our long-haired creep froze, then slowly lifted his hands in the air. I grabbed his long greasy hair and dragged him out to his vehicle, a clapped out old Dodge van. When he was inside, I told him never to come back here if he valued his life!"

"Okay, Betz, so is there something I can do?"

"I hate losing good booze over a creep like this guy." She lifted her head and looked deep into my eyes. A bit of revenge would be nice. Maybe if this little asshole is connected to this other Russian you're looking for?"

"I'll mention your loss to the cops... But I should tell you that the guy who braced your girls is dead. I brought him in for kidnapping a local girl and he died in his jail cell. Someone apparently gave him a suicide pill or something"

Betsy laughed at that. "Alright, Holman, I owe you one. I'll be taking two-hundred off your tab, so your next visit or so will be on the house! But you know those Baptist bastards in the sheriff's office would love to see me leave town! Don't waste your time asking them to help me."

"Betsy, you are a citizen. And they're sworn to serve and protect all citizens of Texas and especially this county."

"Yeah, right, Holman! They care about me and my business?"

"Betsy, a crime was committed here. It's called racketeering, and it's a federal crime, right up there with the kidnapping I'm working on."

The woman smiled at me. "You're a good man, Dave Holman… and a good customer and a friend." She patted my hand to dismiss me. I got in my car and headed back to the city limits.

CHAPTER SIXTEEN

The checkers at the HEB couldn't give me any help, the same with Walmart. Dan Parker out at Winery on the Bay told me he thought the man had been in once or twice. "This guy bought a tasting, four samples for three dollars, but only sampled the high alcohol desert wines, Ice Wine and Port, then he complained that the bottles were overpriced," Dan remembered. "But the guy came back a week later to sample more port. He made me feel a bit uneasy. His eyes held me in an intense stare the whole time he stood at the counter. I was glad when he finally paid his tab and left. As I recall, he didn't leave any tip."

Finally, at a real estate office that specialized in vacation rentals, I got a solid hit, one of the agents recognized 'Mr. Smith's' photo. I flashed my old LAPD badge quickly and told her I was doing some research into a local crime. I didn't offer any more details. The agent didn't look too close at the bogus badge and agreed to help.

Our Russian had leased a large condominium on Allegro Key, a high priced neighborhood just across Little Bay from town.

Jennifer, the leasing agent, gave me the address of the place, telling me Mr. James Smith was a bachelor from Houston who wanted a place for the season where he could bring his clients and fishing buddies on weekends and sometimes during the week as well.

"James Smith?" I asked. "Did he sound English?"

"Well…" she hesitated. "He did have a strong accent of some

kind..."

I thanked her for her help. As I was fastening the seatbelt in my car, I watched through the window as she picked up the phone excitedly and made a call.

I drove straight to police headquarters to share my new information with Hickok and Bishop, but they had left for the day, going back to Corpus Christi for a meeting. Lola Sanchez made note of the Key Allegro address and promised to have a car assigned to keep tabs on the place until she could reach the feds with the gen.

CHAPTER SEVENTEEN

No one came or went from the Key Allegro address while the Rockport Police stood by in an unmarked van. Detective Sanchez was hesitant to say anything to the federal cops until she saw some indication that the Russians might be using the place. We didn't have enough to ask for a search warrant and I believed that Jennifer at the real estate agency had been well paid to warn her clients if anyone was asking about them.

It was a standoff, to say the least. When the cops pulled their surveillance, I decided it was time for some action of my own. I would need Yolanda in the office as an alibi, so I had her call her friend Beccah. Beccah had helped us out on previous cases involving abused women and I trusted her to assist us on this one. Somewhere down the line if there *were* abused young girls, I figured, she would be a big asset to our investigation.

I collected Beccah from her home out by Copano Bay. As I had instructed, she was dressed in dark clothing just as I was. I had my lock picks, a flash light and a small digital camera just in case. We drove out onto Allegro Key, but parked in the lot of the Grog Bar, by the island's yacht harbor. It was only a block or two to the address Jennifer had given me. We pulled on purple-colored medical gloves and crept along the canal side of the properties rather than be seen on the one main street that ran the development's length.

We passed a couple small sailboats docked behind houses as we crept along the seawall. At one dock, where there was a large Boston Whaler tied, we tripped some kind of laser beam and flooded the docks with bright light, but no one emerged from the mansion paired with the dock to check on us or their craft.

The address we were seeking was easy to spot. It was the one with an unkempt, overgrown lawn and a pile of vodka bottles along the back deck. Fences along either side of the property were covered in scarlet-flowered bougainvilleas that added to the location's seclusion. I sidled carefully around to the front, snagging my shirt on the sharp points of the scarlet bushes along the narrow passageway. A small green lizard seemed to mock me from atop the fence. In the front, I checked the address just to make sure. We had the right place.

The back door lock was a special Medico brand which took a heavier key and was advertised as pick proof. The window just down the deck from the back door had no lock at all and had been left partially open. I lifted the glass out of the frame and entered, motioning for Beccah to meet me at the back door.

I walked through the back dining area into the large, open kitchen, where I unlocked the door to the back deck and invited Beccah inside. We gave each other a silent high-five and headed down the hall to the living area of the abode.

There were three bedrooms, two on one side of the passageway and a master suite on the other. The first bedroom was grungy, smelling of unwashed men. Old mattresses littered the floor and ratty sleeping bags covered the mattresses. I recognized Vlad's Russian heavy-metal tee shirt laid out on one of the makeshift bunks.

The next bedroom had home-made, rough wood bunks affixed to the walls. The bunks, stacked three high, had shackles bolted at each end. Some of the sheets had been soiled with urine. The entire room smelled of filth and fear, but there was no one being held there.

The master suite was a whole different story. A king sized bed was made up with silken sheets and a large regal desk stood before the window facing onto the street. There was a set of chains ending in hand cuffs hanging from the ceiling in one corner, and a desktop computer glowed atop the broad desk, but again, no sign of life.

When I tried to log on to the computer, the screen told me that there were no files. The hard drive had been wiped clean. I almost expected a "gotcha" message to pop up just to rub my nose in their disappearance.

Beccah and I went over the rest of the place with a fine tooth comb. We delved through closets and cupboards and combed the soiled sheets for clues while taking pictures of everything as we went. The only clue we came up with was a high school ID card wedged between a mattress and bed frame. The card, issued by Rockport-Fulton High School, bore a picture of a chubby face with the name Sandy Castillo. When we pulled the card out, we found the word "Help" crudely scrawled on the sheets in blood.

I was furiously snapping pictures of the sad message when a car stopping out front caught our attention. I pocketed the camera and we beat a quick retreat out the back door. From the edge of the canal, we watched as a Rockport Police officer walked up the drive, shown his flash light across the front of the house, then got back in his cruiser and drove away.

We hugged each other. Beccah was shaking as we made our retreat back along the inland waterway to the parking lot of Grog. Once in the car, we both breathed a deep sigh of relief and I drove us back to Beccah's place.

CHAPTER EIGHTEEN

O f course there wasn't much I could tell the authorities, as we'd entered the premises illegally, but I tried to get Lola Sanchez's interest anyway. I had prints of all the photos we had shot in the hous but the Rockport Police detective wouldn't even look at them.

"You're telling me that you committed a burglary and violated someone's private residence! Holman, I don't want to hear this. And I most certainly do not want to see solid proof of your indiscretions."

"But we have good evidence that whoever rented that place was holding young girls against their will!"

"Evidence that we *cannot* present in a court of law, David! How many years were you a policeman? You know as well as I do that we can't just run roughshod over the landscape and do as we please. There are procedures that have to be followed!"

"And while we follow procedure, innocent young girls are being used by ruthless criminals, exported as product to be sold to men in other lands…"

"Enough! I don't want to hear it! Our system is based on law and order, and human rights. These men have…"

"These men have innocent young girls, daughters of law abiding citizens, whether they are here legally or not. They aren't playing by any rules, why should we have to…"

Lola Sanchez threw her hands over her ears. "Shut up, Holman! Enough! I don't like this any more than you do! I'll talk to this Jennifer at the rental agency and see if I can't get something that might justify a search warrant. But if it comes out that you creeped the place all bets are off! I'm sorry, but if the FBI guys get wind of your little search, I'll have to go along with them and take you totally off the case. That's it!"

Back at the office, Beccah was having a cup of tea with Yolanda. Neither of them was wearing a happy face. Beccah had counseled too many abused females; girls raped by religious fathers, wives beaten up by drunken husbands and victims of college dates that turned ugly. We all agreed that something had to be done, and we prayed that somehow, the law would step up. But we also agreed that we would, ourselves, take whatever action was necessary if the police wouldn't act on it.

As I drove Beccah home, we discussed what we knew of the case and what law enforcement had done so far.

"I trust you to do whatever has to be done, Dave," Beccah told me. "I think of you as my big brother. You are a very old soul, Dave, and you are dedicated to doing what is right. That's why the police in Los Angeles had to let you go. They couldn't trust you to keep the Blue Code of Silence when fellow officers stepped over the line. They knew, just as I know, that you will do what's right no matter what the cost to you."

CHAPTER NINETEEN

In the morning, I decided to take a beach walk meditation before I put any alcohol into my system. I needed to sort out what I knew in my mind against what was going on around me. There had to be a way to rescue these young ladies within the framework of the law and do it quickly.

If not, I had to find a way to do it all on my own, using only my own limited resources. Yolanda and I could only do so much, even with Beccah's help.

Maybe I could call some cowboy cops I knew in L.A that would take time off and fly down just for the fun of a good fight. We'd have to come up with some quick answers when it was all over, but at least we'd save some of these kids.

Of course, that wasn't a realistic scenario. I was already too deeply involved and I'd be the first name to pop up when the smoke cleared.

The water on Rockport Beach was calm as glass. Small mullet swam around my ankles and flat head catfish jumped from the surface a few feet beyond where I stood. Large blue crabs scurried out of my path as I walked forward. It was the kind of day that made you wonder how anything could be wrong with the world.

But that little voice in the back of my head kept nagging that something *was* wrong in the world.

Mothers with young daughters built sand castles and caught hermit crabs by the water's edge, and that brought me back to reality. All these young children, what were their odds of growing up safe in a world where predators grabbed teens off the streets.

I emptied my pockets on the edge of the sand, cell phone, wallet and car keys, then walked out to where the water got deeper. I dived in over my head, rolled over and floated on my back with eyes closed, and when I'd had enough, I swam back to the deserted area where I'd parked my belongings.

But when I arrived at that spot, by the fourth palapa from the fishing pier, the Russian with the bloody stumps where fingers should have been, stood waiting.

"Mr. Holman! What did you think of my house? No, don't lie, my friends told me they saw you and some dark, ugly woman going in and searching around.

"I am, of course, not happy with this. We need to talk again!"

From behind me in the water, a dark figure with a crossbow style spear gun popped up and dug the tip of his dart into my back. The man had probably been there for awhile, but I hadn't paid any attention. Fishermen with spear guns were common along Aransas Bay. Looking around me, I saw that he was the only person for quite a distance along the sand. The small family had left. No witnesses to question my predicament.

The diminutive Russian cackled. "Come, Mr. Holman, let's go back to my house on Allegro Key. It is quiet there and we can have a little talk." He handed me my wallet and keys, keeping my cell phone out of my reach. When I'd pocketed my things, he grinned and sucker punched me in my solar plexus. Spear gun must have dropped his weapon. He caught me in strong arms and dragged me, coughing and gagging, to a white Mercedes parked just over the dunes. The man belted me into the back seat, leering a rotten-toothed grin and breathing sewer breath on me, then dumped himself behind the wheel in front of me. His Russian boss squeezed into the passenger seat, pointed a small automatic in my direction and shouted, "vpered," which I assumed to mean "go."

The young man with the bad teeth drove the speed limit up Broadway along Little Bay then across the hump-back bridge to Key Allegro. All the way, three-fingers never took his eyes or his gun off me. His evil grin seemed frozen in place. The car turned right onto Curlew Drive, then right again onto Bimini. As we approached the rental property, the garage door opened automatically to welcome us.

In the garage, the driver once again found his spear gun and used it to prod me up a short set of steps into the main room of the house. I was marched back to the room where Beccah and I had seen the crude bunk beds. Spear gun latched a cuff from the lowest bunk around my right ankle, pushed me back to sit on the bottom bed and left the room.

I waited some time, maybe fifteen minutes, maybe half an hour, before the Russian boss man came to see me.

"Mr. Holman, Mr. Holman," he tsked. "Why are you such a difficult man? You have been warned, you have been threatened. In a show of good faith, we returned the young lady you were seeking to her mother. What more can we do?" He slowly shook his head, as though talking to a misbehaving dog. "Have you no sense of self preservation? Do you not understand when you are poking at something too powerful for you to deal with? Why do you persist to be a thorn in my side?"

"I guess I just want to find some answers," I told him honestly.

"Mr. Holman, it would seem that you are just too curious."

"Curiosity is my biggest failing." I grinned.

He backhanded my grin, and when I opened my eyes, the man was not smiling. "You will stop being curious!" he screamed at me. "You will stop it now or it will cost you your life!"

"So be it," I replied more philosophically than I really felt.

He slapped me, hard, first one side of my face and then the other. "This is not good enough!" he shouted, spraying my face with his dirty spittle. "You will stop your investigation into what we are doing, now! You will not be warned again! If you do not go away, we will start hurting people close to you. Eventually, we will kill you, but first you will see people you love die… slowly. You will not be warned again!"

The man turned on his heel and left the room. I sat on my bunk and contemplated the iron ring around my ankle. If I had a tooth pick or a bobby pin, I could probably pick the primitive lock.

As I sat assessing my situation, bad breath with the spear gun came down the hall. He was carrying some kind of large metal canister. I heard a liquid splash from the end of the hall then watched as he passed my door again traveling the other direction. This time the can was tipped over and something pungent was spilling along the hall carpet. A moment after he disappeared from sight I heard a loud whoosh and watched as flames exploded from the passage floor.

In a panic, I started jerking at my restraint. I set my opposite foot against the edge of the bed frame and kicked as hard as I could.

As the wood of the bunk splintered, a loud explosion propelled me backward out the room's window and into the canal behind the house.

Surfacing from the warm water, I could swear I heard someone, somewhere laughing at me. I hardened my resolve. I would never give up until I had these men off the streets and picking cotton for the state of Texas.

CHAPTER TWENTY

Lola Sanchez loosened the wet blankets around me as we sat on the small lawn watching the Rockport Volunteer Firemen drizzle water on the smoldering foundation of the rental house where I had been chained less than an hour before. Some of my hair had been singed off and I was still shivering, but it wasn't at all cold here. The canal had been like bath water, so it must be shock. I watched, mesmerized, as the crimson and blue emergency lights bounced off the bright red of the surrounding bougainvilleas.

Oddly enough, my cell phone sat on the seawall only inches away. I tilted my head towards it and Detective Sanchez picked it up with a puzzled look and handed it to me. The screen said I had one message.

Pushing the glowing button, I was met by the Russian's now familiar voice. "Don't forget, Holman. You drop this case and say no more or people close to you start dying!"

I squinted up at Lola Sanchez to rub it in, "You know this fire destroyed a ton of evidence that could have put this investigation on the right track, don't you?"

"Don't go there, Holman," she hissed. "You know my hands were tied."

"By procedures you have to follow, yeah, I know. But if you just would have gone out on a limb with me... Have I ever steered you wrong?"

"Shut up; just don't go there, Dave." She shook her head and I could see something wet in her eye. "You know I want these monsters…. Probably just as bad as you do, but when we have them on the stand, when we get them, when we *finally* get them and bring them in, and you know we will, I don't want any excuse for some big, well paid attorney to cry foul. I don't want to hurt our case against these freaks by any kind of tainted or inadmissible evidence."

A dark, non-descript sedan pulled up close behind the Fire Chief's car, spitting out two slender forms. Hickok and Bishop came gingerly across the ember littered lawn to join Lola and me at the canal's edge. The two men looked at Lola and then looked at each other. Finally, Hickok turned his eyes to me.

"I'm sorry, Holman," he told me. "Sorry that you've been victimized a time or two for trying to help us."

I could hear the 'but' coming.

"You know you should have left this to us. We're the professionals. We're trained in this kind of thing and we're well paid to take such risks. Do you even have a paying client at this point?"

"I've got training," I told him. "I graduated near the top of my class from the Los Angeles Police Academy and I've had a few courses at Quantico over the years as well. It's not like I'm some novice off the street!"

"Ah, yes, Holman," he replied a bit sheepishly, "we've checked your record.

"But you're not working for any government agency at this point. And, from what I understand, you've been doing some illegal checking as well, breaking and entering, maybe a class one felony? Stuff like that..."

"Yeah, and I've gotten the hair burned off my head for my efforts. That's about as far as you can see. Never mind that I found the dungeon where young kidnapped girls have been held, proven that someone is kidnapping the daughters of immigrants and poor rednecks and taken a beating or two for my troubles. Or the fact that I've been face-to-face with this menace you seem reluctant to go up against."

"Mr. Holman," Hickok's sidekick Bishop offered. "With all due respect, we've been working hard to pin these people to our board, so to speak. We've run their profiles and searched their background. We've looked for patterns that could aid us in putting them into the computer to ultimately corner them in a box."

"Yeah, right," I sneered. "How about we look at their Face Book profiles, see how many cute kitten videos they've posted!"

"Social media *does* often yield some interesting clues into the criminal psyche..." Hickok began.

"Enough!" I shouted. "We know we have a gang of Russians, former KGB officers gone rogue, that are set on taking advantage of lax American law enforcement in order to build a criminal empire much like Italian immigrants did during prohibition..."

"I hardly think you can call us lax...." Hickok tsked. "Maybe a bit over stretched."

"Right," Detective Sanchez said. "And we were so happy to see the Berlin Wall come down that..."

"Don't even go there," Bishop interrupted. "None of this bickering is helping us. The bottom line is a gang of criminals has been running us around in circles. Maybe we've missed some opportunities by following the rules too closely."

This statement earned him a dropped-jaw look from his FBI boss. "But we now know that they are running scared. They've burned down their *own* safe house. They continue to warn off the one civilian detective that is on to them in an effort to be rid of their most believable witness.

"I think Dave Holman is our key in bringing these people to justice."

Lola Sanchez gave an affirmative nod.

"Mr. Holman, would you mind working with us in the form of a bit of bait to draw these criminals closer to prosecution?"

Hickok's expression said, "No, this isn't how we work," but my broad grin settled the matter. "I'm in," I grinned, "Myself, my partner Yolanda and all my staff!"

"You understand what you're up against?" Hickok said.

"Yeah, yeah," I answered. "So does Yolanda and Beccah and all our other helpers. I'm an old man. What are our lives worth if we can't provide a safe future for innocent young girls with all their years ahead of them?"

Hickok coughed loudly, but Lola Sanchez smiled, reached out and squeezed my hand. I thought about Humphrey Bogart in Casablanca; "I'm no good at being noble, but it doesn't take much to see that the problems of three little people don't amount to a hill of beans in this crazy world." I almost said it out loud, but thought better of it. The Rockport locals already believed I was a brick or two short of a load.

CHAPTER TWENTY-ONE

Yolanda pulled up shortly after that, concern in her eyes and love too. I could see Beccah waiting in Yolanda's VW Thing, empathy in her dark, piercing eyes as well.

Yolanda assured all that I would be down at the station early in the morning to make a full statement, but the policemen at the scene already knew that. I parked my dripping clothes and body in the Thing's back seat and we headed for the office. I needed to do some serious brainstorming on this case. Was Rockport Beach safe to walk? The bad guys had grabbed me from there twice.

I knew a clear head was a big advantage for working these things out, but at the same time I was smarting from the beatings I'd taken at the hands of these clowns.

"As soon as I change clothes," I told Yolanda, "I think we should go up to Rusty's. I'll buy you a beer or two and we'll try to dissect just what's wrong with this case. Beccah, I'll buy you a Coke as well if you want to join us."

Yolanda gave me a questioning look; as in questioning my sanity, but she nodded agreement. Beccah said she'd had enough drama for one day and asked that we take her home first.

There was a football game on the television behind the bar. Rusty had the sound turned up and the gathered crowd was engrossed in the action on the big screen. I steered Yolanda to a table in the far corner where we could almost hear each other without shouting.

Brenda, the red-head afternoon waitress came to take our orders. From the way she was staring at me I could tell she wanted to ask why my hair and eyebrows were mostly gone, but she didn't say a word about it. I asked for my usual Redfish IPA, then thought a minute and ordered a double shot of Jameson's Irish on the side. Yolanda didn't even blink, she knows me too well. She ordered a gin and tonic for herself.

"How many young girls are out there?" I asked rhetorically when Brenda had gone back to the bar. "How many have already been taken beyond our reach and how many do we still have a chance to save?" I felt my eyes growing moist, whether from the stress of the day or the thought of lost lives, I couldn't say. I took a few deep breaths as I looked into Yolanda's serious face.

She got out of her chair, came around the table and gave me a hug, her own orbs moist as well.

"You are a good man, Dave Holman! Sometimes I think you might be too sensitive for the kind of work you've chosen to do..."

"Hey, this is the work I do." I countered. "If I hadn't seen the jungles of Asia and all the suffering there at such a young, tender age, I might have taken another path..."

Yolanda put her hand over mine as she sat back down in her chair. "Dave, don't! Don't go there. That was a long time ago!"

"Yeah, and so were the Rodney King riots, and the O J Riots. But they are all imprinted on my memory, just a little too strong to forget! All those people, human brothers and sisters out there being blamed and mistreated, losing their homes and businesses to a mob violence mentality. And I was an authority figure that was supposed to be able to help them! I did what I could, but...."

"That was then, Dave," Her dark brown orbs locked into mine. "You survived all those things. They left scars, but they made you a stronger man as well. And right now you need to call on all that strength. You, we, are dealing with very bad people, people with no morals or conscience, and you are the man that's strong enough, brave enough... Man enough to defeat them! So let's talk about a plan!"

As I sat there locked into Yolanda's stare, I felt more than saw someone pull out the chair next to me. "Holman," the man spoke, "I am not assigned to this case you're working on, but I want to help in any way I can."

I turned my head to find a young man, probably in his twenties, with a blond buzz-cut and muscular arms seated to my right. I'd seen him somewhere before.

"Sheriff's Department?"

He extended a hand across to me. "Deputy Sam Carlson. I've read all the notes on the computer. A cousin of mine down in Corpus has a neighbor that recently lost a daughter."

I turned to face the man. "Tell me about it."

"My cousin says his neighbor's girl was kind of a wild child, but she wasn't the type to just run off with some stranger. I've met her a few times myself. She's a sweet kid and I agree with the family.

The Corpus Christi cops looked at it for a day or two and announced that she was just an out-of-control teenager. They put further investigation on a very low priority, but I believe the girl was kidnapped. Her boyfriend hasn't heard a word from her. She had been going steady with him for almost two years! So who did she run away with?"

I looked at Yolanda and she gave a slight nod "yes." We should trust this man and work with him.

"We can't bring you in officially," I told the man, "but I'll pay you as an operative in your off-duty hours. Will that work for you, Carlson?"

"I don't expect to get paid," he told us. "I just want to help find out what happened to this girl. I want to bring these people some closure about their daughter's fate."

"Dave?" Yolanda questioned. "Can't you talk to the sheriff and maybe get Sam assigned to the case? I know the sheriff's department is taking an interest as well."

"I could do that. Would that work for you, Carlson?"

The young man broke out in a wide grin. "That would be just about perfect." He replied, "But I'm only working patrol, would an assignment like that require me to be a detective grade?"

"Dave can handle it," Yolanda told the man, reaching across the table to pat his hand.

"Ex-marine?" I asked.

"Two tours, Bagdad and Afghanistan," The man replied.

CHAPTER TWENTY-TWO

We bought Sam Carlson a plate of grouper and a beer while I filled him in on recent happenings. The young man produced a thin reporter-style notebook from his shirt pocket and scrawled the pertinent facts on its pages.

I had three or four more Redfish Ales with some crawfish pies before Yolanda announced that I should be cut off. Brenda grinned at me, but brought the check without another glass of alcohol. Yolanda liberated a MasterCard from my pocket and settled the tab, then put her arm around my shoulders to guide me into her VW Thing.

I snuck another shot or two from the office bottle while Yolanda was in the bathroom. It was starting to get dark outside. I closed my eyes for a moment to try to clear my head and when I opened them, bright sunshine was assaulting me. I must have slept for nine or ten hours!

Yolanda brought strong coffee and garlic Nan bread. My body felt stiff from sleeping at my desk, but after a few hits of the java, I felt pretty good. Certainly well enough to go down to the cop shop and make my statement about the day before! Lola Sanchez was there when I arrived. She ushered me into the back conference room where the FBI guys waited, then summoned the uniforms who were first on the scene at the fire in Allegro Key when I had been rescued. The Chief of Police also joined our little confab, interested in what the consequences of a Russian mob house for kidnapped girls on his patch might bring.

We quickly agreed that the Rockport Police bore no responsibility at the outset. How could anyone know such a thing was occurring? On the other hand, once we had such knowledge, it became a duty to deal with these people swiftly and with whatever force necessary.

I assured the Chief that I was part of his team and would say nothing that could dump the Rockport or Aransas County teams into the shit. My only interest with this case was in seeing that treating young girls like some kind of product to be sold and used was halted as quickly as possible, and that the monsters who had such small regard for human life and dignity be strapped to a state gurney and given a lethal needle for their trouble. That got a smile and a nod from the two uniforms.

"The guy they keep sending as a messenger to me," I told the assembled cops, "Seems to have lost two of his fingers as discipline for screwing up, but they didn't kill him."

"Chelnikov!" Hickok breathed. I nodded.

"That tells me he must be someone important. Not one of the elite officers in this business, but all the same, someone they need to keep working for them, someone they don't want to lose."

"He was a pilot. Probably still is!" Bishop repeated. "If he's the main, or the more likely the only, pilot they trust to move them around…"

"And he seems to be useful as an errand boy as well," I added.

"And if none of the other higher-ups know how to fly a plane or a helo…" Hickok mused. "Yes, he would be too valuable to purge. It makes sense."

We agreed that someone from the city or county would tail me to try and capture Chelnikov. In the meantime, I would move forward with my own investigation and report all I found to both the feebs and the locals. One way or another, we'd take these bad men off the board.

CHAPTER TWENTY-THREE

I returned to the office to find a distraught Yolanda holding the telephone to her ear while her other hand drummed fingers on the desktop.

"How can this be? I thought you'd have Sammi in Tennessee by now, almost to Hohenwald and the sanctuary!"

I gave a confused look and she pushed the button to put the phone in speaker mode. Darpaknu's voice came forth loud and clear. "We stopped for a day outside Houston," he replied in a shaky voice. "Budhan has a girlfriend there that teaches the third grade and she wanted the children in her school to meet a real live elephant. Sammi loved playing with the children and the principal told us we could camp on the school's playground for the night. It is all fenced, so Sammi could roam around and get some exercise before we got back on the road." His trembling voice sounded close to tears.

"Just a minute," Yolanda told him. "Dave is here now. I want to fill him in on what has happened."

Unnecessarily putting her hand over the receiver, Yolanda turned to me. "Darpaknu tells me Sammi has been kidnapped, along with Budhan and Payush. He parked the truck somewhere between Houston and Port Arthur, a little town called Anahuac, and went into a roadside diner to get takeout meals for everyone. While he was paying for the food, he saw the truck pulling out onto the highway. Someone he didn't know was driving and he thought he saw Butthead and Payush lying in the truck bed with Sammi."

She took her hand off the instrument's mouthpiece. "Dar, do you still have the Rescue's credit card?"

"Of course, Yo, I was buying the food for us with it." His voice was returning to a more normal timbre.

"Listen to me, Darpaknu," Yolanda told him in a slow careful voice. "Call the local police and report what happened. Tell them everything you can remember about the truck being stolen. When you're finished filing the report, ask them to help you find a rental car agency."

"File a police report and then go to a place and rent a car," the young man repeated dutifully.

"Yes," Yolanda began again. "And when you have the car, drive straight back here to Rockport. It's just over two hundred miles, so you should be back here late tonight and you can report everything you remember to Dave."

"One other thing I did not tell you," the man said in slightly happier voice. "Butthead's girlfriend said she wanted to know exactly where he was at all times and she put a little bug thing on the bumper of the truck. She said she would track us on her computer and I asked if I could see how it worked. She let me copy the software onto my laptop."

"So do you think I can find this program?" Yolanda asked hesitantly, "so Dave might be able to track Sammi and the boys?"

"No, you will not need to." Excitement was blossoming in Darpaknu's voice. "I had brought my computer into the restaurant so I could check my email while I waited for our meals. I have the software and you can follow Sammi on my machine as soon as I get there! Wait, I am booting up right now...."

Yolanda spun a Bic pen around the tabletop with her fingernail as I continued to stare at the telephone, wishing I had a drink. After what seemed like an hour, Darpaknu came back on the speakerphone. "It looks like our truck is headed back around the bay toward Houston!" he exclaimed.

I leaned over the speaker phone. "Okay, Darpaknu. Just get with the police as quick as you can, get a vehicle and get back here. I'll know what to do when I see what you've got."

"Yes," Yolanda told him. "Hurry up and file a police report then get back here as quick as you can!"

CHAPTER TWENTY-FOUR

Darpaknu knocked on the office door not long after midnight.

"The Anahuac police sent me to the Harris County sheriff's office. They said they were short handed and because we were only passing through...."

"But you got a copy of their report, right?"

Darpaknu produced three pages of yellow carbonless carbon paper from his laptop bag, handed them to me and then drew his computer out.

We had him place his small laptop on my desk as we opened the tracer program Butthead's girlfriend had downloaded for him. The icon for Sammi's truck had not moved far from the point where our crew had been hijacked. The small glowing truck shape blinked off and on just down the Houston Ship Channel, a short ways south of Pasadena, Texas. We talked about what had happened, keeping the screen up for maybe two hours without the little red truck shape ever moving.

The office phone woke us up early the next morning. Caller ID simply said "out-of-area." Yolanda answered by punching the speaker phone button. Before we could say a word of greeting a heavily accented voice blared forth warning me to back off my investigation if I wanted the elephant and my two helpers to be released unharmed.

"If you continue to be a thorn in my side," the seemingly familiar voice continued, "We will torture the elephant in front of his little brown friends and then kill them as well. We might even consider bringing your brown lady friend here to watch us torture your elephant. She is a bit, how do you say, long of nose, to bring a good price on the girlie market, but we might even find someone who will buy your friend. Maybe we can arrange to send you videos of what our clients might choose to do with her? Are you getting any of this, Mr. Holman? Do you understand the business we mean?

"Worthless young girls are none of *your* business, Mr. Holman! What does it take to show this to you? Is interrupting the business of my friends worth losing this beast and two or more of your friends?" The phone's small speaker erupted into maniacal laughter, which ended abruptly when the man on the other end pushed the button to hang up. We had never gotten a word in on our end.

Yolanda and I looked at each other. Darpaknu came into the room buttoning his shirt. "Last night, I fixed up my little recorder to your phone," he told us. "If you should wish to listen to this conversation again, I have a tape in the little machine under your desk." He knelt down and pointed to a black box dangling by twist ties from the center drawer.

I surprised the dark-skinned little man with a bear hug. "Dar. You are amazing!" I told him. "I may not want to hear this conversation again, but it will be fun to replay it for the police."

And it was fun! The FBI guys confiscated the copy of the tape I brought them immediately to analyze it and make copies. "We'll hold onto this for you," Hickok told me. Our Rockport chief demanded a transcription ASAP. "And one for the sheriff too!" he called after them.

When the meeting was back in order, I brought out Darpaknu's laptop and shared the ingeniousness of Budhan's girlfriend's truck tracking along with the police report from Harris County. The chief had a call placed to Harris County requesting their cooperation and filling them in on the big picture and the tie-in of the previous day's kidnapping with the local investigation into the Russian criminals.

Hickok and Bishop immediately fired up their own computers, scanning Google maps of the area where Darpaknu's computer put our truck and baby elephant. They quickly zoomed in on the Houston Channel real estate, then set to work pin-pointing ownership of various tracts of land along the length of the waterway.

They found that a few acres along the east side of the channel had recently been purchased by a Ukrainian oil exploration company. There was a small tank farm on the land, but no indication that it was actively being used. The more they checked the internet about the site, the more suspicious it appeared.

There was a tanker dock along much of the property's waterfront, but the only vessel their maps showed was some kind of bulky old derelict craft, not something that could move crude oil around. On satellite photos the old vessel appeared to be run up on a tiny finger of beach to the south of the docking piers. It was a wide and blunt-ended vessel, nothing like any of the other ships in this mostly industrial area.

I made copious mental notes of the tract of land, its coordinates and the roads leading to it. I tried to memorize the layout of boats and buildings as the feds and locals discussed what all this might mean and how to best check it out. While they talked about surveillance and warrants, I made up my mind to drive up to Houston and out to the ship channel area to surprise my enemies before they could guess what was coming. I didn't need any warrants. I needed to rescue one elephant and a pair of workers that were good friends to my special lady. And after that, I needed to be sure that a net of law enforcement people closed tightly around them.

"Holman?" I heard Hickok call, "are you listening?"

"Oh yeah, sure," I piped up. "I'm right there with you."

We shared cell phone numbers and I promised to stay out of it, but to stay in touch while the FBI set up a listening post near our query and made their plans to raid the Russian property.

"No cowboy stuff, Holman," Bishop told me with serious eyes. "We don't want you screwing this up for us. Just stay in your office and let us know if you hear anything from the Russians. We'll do this thing by the book and professionally, and when it's all over, we'll see that you get whatever credit is due in breaking the case."

I smiled and gave a positive nod. Yeah, right, I thought. Like they're going to look out for an elephant and a couple young men that might get in their way. I'd have my meeting with Yolanda when I left here and we'd make realistic plans to protect our own. Chances are we'd get it all done and hand it to the feds on a pretty dish. If not, we'd probably die defending our own and the thousands of young girls out there at risk.

And if we did die, well, at least it might fan the fires to insure some real justice in this thing.

"You're good with this, Holman?" the Rockport chief asked.

"Of course," I smiled back. "I'm just happy to be here."

CHAPTER TWENTY-FIVE

It was well after midnight when I finally hit the road for Houston. Darpaknu had printed out maps and plats of the entire eastern bank of the Houston ship channel. We had viewed the area on Google Maps as closely as we could, then enlarged those frames until we could almost count grains of sand on the beach.

"I'm going to check this out solo, on my own," I proclaimed. "I'll stay closely in touch with you, Yo," I told her. "If I need help, the FBI or you and Beccah can track me and do what needs to be done. These people have already make threats against you. I don't want to give them any opportunity."

I thought about it for a minute. "I'd like it if you went to Beccah's place for the time I'm gone. Forward the office phone over there as well. We will stay in touch, but I don't want you to be at risk. These people know where we live. It would be just like them to break down the door here and grab you as another pawn in their game!"

Yolanda began to protest, but I silenced her with a scowl. "You know what happened when Reverend Clemson kidnapped you and took you to Port Aransas. I don't want you suffering like that again if I can help it!"

Yolanda replied, "Of course, Dave," but I sensed that she had plans of her own forming behind her pretty smile.

"I'm serious, Yo!" I stated emphatically. "This is my case and I'm the man. *I* do the heavy lifting here and you man the office. You have a collection of public agencies that you can call to help me if I get into a situation!"

"Of course, Dave," she repeated, suppressing a wicked grin. I could only hope that she would take my concerns seriously. I packed some bottles of water and sandwiches in the Saab, along with an empty milk carton and a sleeping bag in case this turned into a lengthy surveillance. I thought about bringing my old Walther PP along for self defense, but decided it would be pretty worthless against an army of thugs. Even if I was able to shoot one or two of them, I probably wouldn't get out of there alive. Stealth was my best weapon.

I finally hit 35 North driving toward Houston with some reservations about the whole plan. I encountered some bad thunderstorms just north of Port Lavaca with rain so heavy I had to keep my wipers on the highest setting for more than ten miles. By Bay City, the rain had cleared and I had smooth sailing until I saw the sun rising over Pearland.

I found an International House of Pancakes just south of Houston, where I ate a big breakfast, then I pulled off the road, dropped the Saab's driver seat back and took a short powernap in a Walmart parking lot. When I woke up, I followed Interstate 45 along the Houston ship channel toward the Gulf, carefully observing the shoreline on the other side of the big, dirty ditch and comparing it to what I had memorized from the Google images. In this manner I was able to locate the empty docks and tank farm owned by the so-called Russian oil company.

I saw no activity in the area. The large blunt-ended vessel from the satellite scans appeared to be an antique car ferry, the kind that used to cross the Hudson River from New York to Hoboken, New Jersey. Were there really any of those left outside marine museums? And where had this one come from?

I backtracked toward the city, found a place to cross over the channel and then made a slow cruise down the east bank, easing past the Russian property while closely observing the territory. When I had a good idea of where gates, buildings and boundaries were located, I drove north through Pasadena to San Jacinto where the old battleship Texas was docked as a monument. I always enjoyed touring old ships and found them interesting and relaxing. Checking out how World War II sailors lived would take my mind off the case for an hour or two and help regroup my thoughts.

I paid my admission and walked the decks of the USS Texas until the sun was sinking. Just after dark, I had a big dinner and a couple gin and tonics in a Pasadena restaurant. It was a little after 9:00 when I headed back down Route 3 on the channel's east side.

There were some lights on at the Russian oil depot. Sodium vapor floodlights illuminated the docks, with one or two more along the outer perimeter near the road. A faint glow came from the windows of one or two buildings in the gated area. I drove a half mile farther on and parked my Saab beside the road near the gates to a huge Exxon facility. I dressed in black jeans, a black long-sleeved tee shirt and my old dark blue Coast Guard watch cap, smearing some smoky shoe black on my hands and face.

I walked back up the road in a crouch, keeping to the ditch on the outside of the road. I flattened myself on the ground each time a vehicle passed, mostly large tank trucks. I didn't see any police presence in the area. From time to time I climbed up from the roadside ditch to the edge of the asphalt and checked my bearings, then dropped back down out of sight.

On one of my looks around, I thought I saw the outline of a Volkswagen Thing coming down the road, but that couldn't be. Or could it? But then again, how many VW Things were out there in the world?

Not many, I reasoned, but still there had to be some. In the darkness, I couldn't discern it's age or color. And I'd told Yolanda to stay home and man the office from Beccah's place, so it must be just another old Volkswagen.

CHAPTER TWENTY-SIX

On arriving at the site, I paced the perimeter twice, making a mental note of every inch of the property. In my mind, for a minute, I was back on my little riverboat in the Asian jungles searching for a way to bring Charlie out in the open where we could fry the communist bastards. I shook my head to clear that old memory. I was here, in the here-and-now, here to save vulnerable young women from a life of slavery and degradation.

I found a stretch on the western fence where the razor wire had come loose and sagged down below the top of the chain link fencing. Much of the property looked to be in a serious state of disrepair.

I kept getting the feeling that someone was observing me, but I could see no one on either side of the chain link mesh. I'd already ascertained the absence of any cameras or other security devices that could detect my presence.

I made my move, writing off my uneasy feeling to paranoia. I stepped back a few yards, made a running approach across the deserted highway, leaping up the fence and vaulting to the top. I launched myself off the fence's top rail to make sure I cleared the dangling curls of razor sharp tongues.

I landed hard on the other side, on a tiny asphalt patch peppered with pipes and valves, rolled forward and quickly flattened myself against the tarmac to blend in. A short hiss of steam from one of the nearby pipes almost gave me a heart attack. I stayed still for almost five minutes, massaging my aching knees and hearing nothing; nothing was stirring anywhere around me beyond the occasional trail of vapor from the pipe off to my side.

I cautiously raised my head. I still had that uneasy feeling that someone was keeping an eye on me, but I could find no basis for my suspicions, so I crawled on my belly off the open area and toward the glowing buildings.

The first structure was an ancient Quonset hut set partially in the shadows of the towering tanks. Peering through the front window, I saw nothing but pallets of boxes stacked in neat rows under a single bare light bulb. No living thing moved within that I could ascertain.

Fifty yards on, I came to a square stucco structure just off the quayside. I circled the building cautiously twice, once at a distance, the second time closer up. I could hear raised voices within.

I crept up to a window at the rear and lifted my head to peek inside. Chelnikov was leaning against some shelving on the far wall. He had a half-empty bottle of vodka in one hand as he gesticulated at his audience.

That audience consisted of two young men, with their backs to me and assault rifles slung over their shoulders, one fair haired and one dark. The soldiers listened, but their posture didn't display confidence in their leader. They turned and smirked at each other from time to time. One young man held his hand just under the edge of the desk with his middle finger extended, which brought giggles to his friend and a red apoplectic face from Chelnikov.

I stared transfixed at the scene until the Russian leader sent a glance toward my window and started shouting words I couldn't understand as he waved his vodka bottle around. I turned and beat feet toward the dark area beyond the Quonset hut.

When no one came out of the stucco bungalow, I decided it was safe to continue my inspection of the property. I circled to the side of the old tin hut shaded by the tanks from the perimeter lights to have a peek in the rear windows. The glass was covered with dark curtains, but some light escaped from a rent in the fabric.

I eased myself up to peer through the torn fabric and almost gave myself away with my loud, sharp intake of breath. More ramshackle bunks like those in the Key Allegro house lined the down-curving walls, only these pallets held pitiful looking creatures in torn bits of clothing. It was like those old photographs from the liberation of Nazi death camps but instead of old Jewish men, these beds held young girls in their teens.

I now knew I had to get Hickok and Bishop in here as quickly as possible, but decided to scout around just a while longer. I must have a firm grasp of every inch of the landscape if I was to help to coordinate their raid of the facility.

I moved forward cautiously around the old tanks that lined the channel beyond the small buildings. They were in bad shape. So bad I found it hard to believe they would still be useful for storing anything liquid. Parts of their outer walls were covered in rust and large pieces of the metal siding appeared to be peeling away. Potholes along the path were filled with rank smelling chemical mixes.

At the end of the row of storage tanks, I made my way to the extended dockside. Much of the pier was in just as bad a shape as the tanks. There were large gaps where wood planking had fallen through or completely rotted away. Two of the pilings had come loose and leaned drunkenly out toward the dark oily water of the channel. I didn't dare walk out on this failing structure.

Instead, I backtracked through the tank farm until I reached the other end of the broken-down pier. I got down on all fours and crawled toward the aged ferry boat, the last place that I needed to check out. On approaching the vessel I could smell something familiar and foul. Was it elephant dung?

Before I could complete my analysis, I heard a sorrowful moan, recognizable but not quite human. Sammi came to mind! Of course, these people had Sammi here somewhere. I made a hunched-over run for the old boat, jumped onto the car loading ramp and continued on across the wet wooden deck.

CHAPTER TWENTY-SEVEN

From the far side of the deck, I could see a hastily thrown together pen of old piping lashed together with a ton of bailing wire. A mournful looking gray figure huddled within the pen and two sleeping men were handcuffed to a corner section of pipe which was firmly planted in a square of concrete.

Sammi must have recognized my scent. The young elephant let loose with a loud, happy cry that filled the night with her joy. The two huddled figures by her pen popped up to look around; Budhan and Payush! Their shackles rattled as they sat up to look in my direction.

I put my finger to my lips, hoping they could see me in the poor light of this corner of the property. One of the men nodded and half stood reaching into the pen to calm the captive pachyderm.

I thought things were copacetic until I heard a loud human bellow from the shoreline. I turned to see Chelnikov and his troopers burst through the door of the small shack back by the pier.

With my options severely limited, I crab-walked to the far end of the old boat and slipped into the oily waters of the channel. I dove under the surface and swam towards the falling down pier. Resurfacing in the shadow of that structure, I clung to one of the pilings and turned my ears to the shoreline.

There was a lot of shouting and a few rounds of automatic weapon fire out over the water. I did a chin-up on the rotting wood attached to the piling and watched as the three Russians stumbled toward the thin strip of sand where the ferry boat rested.

Before they reached the ancient craft, I heard a two-fingered whistle back among the tank farm. A silhouette appeared briefly along the path then, like a phantom, it was gone.

The two young men fired a series of bursts in the direction of the sound, some of their shots striking the chemical puddles and sending up a quick flash of flame, before Chelnikov bellowed a command in Russian and they brought their guns to port arms.

There were more loud shouts and the two men spread out on either side of their leader. The three of them moved forward across the scrub land, rifles swinging back and forth without locating a target. The trio ended up at the Quonset hut where Chelnikov checked the locks and brought out a flashlight to look for signs of forced entry.

A bull-like bellow told me he had found my footprints in the mud under the hut's rear window. The man fished in his pockets for a set of keys and ran around to the front and entered the structure.

He emerged moments later shaking his head and mumbling something I couldn't hear. I guess he was confused but satisfied that all his girls were still in place.

The trio was headed back to their small cabin when there was another series of loud noises from among the old storage tanks. It sounded like a pile of bricks falling followed by a Tarzan-like yodel. The men froze in their tracks for a heartbeat or two, then took off at a clumsy trot toward that area.

The Pachyderm Predicament

Their shift of attention gave me time to pull myself up on the bank and look for shelter. I chose the labyrinth presented by the three decks of the ancient ferry for my hiding place. I climbed the stairs to the passenger deck and crawled to the shore-side edge, where I leaned over the edge to watch what was happening.

By my escape onto the vessel I managed to elude Chelnikov and his boys while they searched along the edge of the water. It was a dark night, just a thin sliver of moon shedding very little light when the clouds allowed it through at all, to supplement the few lights over the landing. They talked in raised voices and waved their weapons around, but in the end, they returned to their air conditioned space away from the humid Texas night.

CHAPTER TWENTY-EIGHT

I decided that it would be suicide to keep bothering these men in their comfortable space and set off to once again check the property beyond the lit-up buildings. I tried to stay downwind of Sammi's pen to avoid another trumpet call from the baby elephant. There was nothing else worth noting, so I made mental notes of all I'd seen to relay to the FBI and the others.

Satisfied that I'd done all I could I decided I'd hide on the beached boat and call in a law enforcement strike on my cell phone. As I wandered the upper decks of the ferry I noted that the vessel looked vaguely like The Islander, the boat my parents used to take me on from San Pedro, California to Terminal Island, in the '50s. It was a craft from that time when there were more pedestrians than cars, a time when every ferry boat had a superstructure over the car-carrying deck with benches for the folks who had no vehicles to sit in.

The wood of the upper decks was cracked and dry, sorely in need of a coat of paint. Warnings and instructions were all in Spanish along the benches and bulkheads, and the metal walls of the boat were coated with a thick patina of rust. It seemed doubtful that this old tub could even float. I crept off the boat and back to where they had Sammi locked in the old pipeline pen. I moved in a crouch to our baby elephant, making cooing, comforting sounds as I approached, but Sammi recognized me again and trumpeted a happy call upon seeing me. At that instant, bright stadium lights came on all around the yard.

The two young men ran forward from the edge of the light holding their machine pistols against their shoulders, ready to fire. The lead man was blond and pear shaped, wearing high-water jeans that only reached the top of his ankles and a filthy macaw-filled Hawaiian shirt with the buttons stretched tight over a voluminous beer gut. His partner looked more like a bear than a man. He wore only baggy brown shorts and sandals. His entire six-foot plus frame was covered with thick black hair. Even his full beard reached up to just below his eyes. The hair on his head was thick and unruly below a sort of stark-white bald monk's crown. I expected Chelnikov to come forward with them but when they had me surrounded, Gorby Sergejevič, Gorby the Gobbler, stepped out into the light.

"Welcome, Mr. Holman, we've been expecting you! I knew you wouldn't disappoint me, but please tell me, where is your little dark elephant girl? Is she back there with you?"

"I told her to stay out of this," I lied. "I told her that I would save her elephant for her and she needn't worry."

The man burst forth with an evil laugh. "Yes, I could almost believe that, Mr. Holman. Except that we know more about your lady than you think. We know that she too is Russian. A Russian Jew! Not the favorite people among our countrymen, but one of us, just the same. We know she is quite tenacious like many Russian women, not the type who gives up or backs down!"

I walked forward across the sandy strip where the man they called Gorby the Gobbler stood and I spit in the man's face, probably a little too impulsive on my part. Strong arms grabbed me from behind and someone forced me to the ground where they put a knee in my back and proceeded to bind my hands with thick strips of Velcro.

"You offend me, Mr. Holman," the old Russian said. "I am just a businessman, trying to do business in your country. *Your* stupid moral code gets in my way, but I look at your politicians, your representatives, they don't seem to worry about these silly issues of morality. I have sold young girls to some of your elected Texas officials, young boys too! What makes you so special that you rebel against what seems a tacitly accepted policy? As long as the common people, the voters, don't know or don't care, why should your law enforcement people care? Are they not paid enough? Do they need more incentives?"

The man placed his right elbow in the palm of his left hand and stroked his cheek with his right hand in a sort of Jack Benny pose. "I think you are some kind of Quixote figure, Mr. Holman, tilting at windmills, as they say. I don't think your government will stand behind you when all this is judged. Your leaders may talk about Christian values, but in truth your politicians are only interested in what pleasures they can enjoy for themselves! They will find a way to bury all this where the media cannot make a big deal of it."

"I think you're full of shit!" I screamed from the ground at the top of my lungs. "You want to believe the world is corrupt because it justifies your lack of care for your fellow human beings! You are the lowest form of scum from the filthiest, most toxic pond of water out there!"

At that, one of the young men stepped forward and swung a two by four block of wood at my face. The pain shot through my head in a blue flash, wiping all consciousness from my mind.

CHAPTER TWENTY-NINE

My next coherent moment was being dragged up a ramp onto the ancient boat, flooding me with youthful memories of the Islander in San Pedro. I was dumped, like a sack of potatoes, against a railing. A thick rope was laced through the Velcro ties on my wrists and double knotted to a docking bollard near the boat's loading ramp. I shook my head violently side to side to bring my full focus back to here and now.

From my resting place I watched them drive our elephant Sammi toward the ferry's car deck. The young pachyderm widened fearful eyes at the lapping water on either side. She didn't want to be moved again. Several times as they pushed her forward, she rebelled and fought. The first time, she almost sat on the dark bear of a man shoving her from behind. On their second attempt, Sammi reared up, pumping her front legs in the air like she was riding a bicycle.

From a small tin shed on the dockside, another man ran forward with a rifle tucked into his shoulder. I screamed, "No!" but the man fired a single shot and I saw Sammi rear up again, then drop her chest to the ground with her back legs extended but her front stretched out, like a Muslim at prayer.

Bear man approached her from the front with a pole. Whacking at her chest, he brought Sammi to her feet, but she swayed woozily, like a drunken sailor.

It took four of them to finally push and prod the baby elephant across the deck and into another smaller pipe pen, where she collapsed in a heap. The bear-like man tossed the pole down on the deck but carried the rifle somewhere into the bowels of the old ferry. The fair haired, pear shaped lackey came over to give me a grin and a kick in the side. When I looked up, he had my cell phone in his hand. With a hearty laugh, he tossed it over the side.

With the elephant on board, pear-shape and hairy went back to drag our bound helpers, Budhan and Payush, onto the boat and then prod them up the stairs to the passenger deck like they were hobbled cattle.

One of my captors dropped down a hatch amidships. After a few minutes, I heard the Ferry's engines cough to life and a faint row of lights came on along the overhead.

The bearded and shirtless dark soldier popped out of the hatch and scurried back to where Gorby Sergejevič stood. He came to attention and gave a crisp salute. I realized that these men must know something about navy life and seafaring. They may not be intent on saving our lives, but they had enough seamanship to sail this old Mexican tub out to a place where the sea would swallow us into oblivion.

I glanced furtively around for some avenue of escape. *Nathan shaken!* And even if I could break my hands free and get away, who was to rescue Sammi!

I felt the boat vibrating under me, then heard steel grating on sand. They had to rev the engines to red-line RPMs to pull us from the sandy beach. With a gargantuan shudder, the vessel broke free and made a leap out toward the channel where it stopped and idled.

We were setting sail from a remote bit of shore in the midst of oil rigs and dirty, soiled sand along the channel that led from Texas

City to Baytown. Everything for miles around was industrial waterfront owned by oil companies and hardly a single human with an eye looking toward the waterway.

As if to accent my doubts, an old military helicopter came overhead, circled a time or two and landed atop the peak of the old craft, near the bridge from which a captain would navigate. Its twirling propellers just barely cleared the top of the ferry's pilot house.

When the rotors slowed, a diminutive figure hopped down onto the roof and climbed down to the main deck. The pilot was Chelnikov. He advanced and gave Gorby a hug. "We are good, so far," He beamed and shouted loudly enough for me to hear from the far end of the lower deck.

As the two men grinned and slapped hands at their good fortune, I suddenly saw Yolanda from the corner of my eye. She was covered in black clothing from head to toe, just like me, as she crept along the shoreline. The moon passed behind a fat cloud and she made a leap, almost falling into the oily waters of the channel, but at the last instant catching the lip of the deck at the back of this rusting bucket and pulling herself aboard. What noise she made was covered by the whine of the rotors still winding down overhead.

My lady hastily scurried into the shadow of one of the low bulkheads that ran along the car deck. As quickly as she appeared, she was gone, somewhere into the depths of the old vessel. For a moment I wondered if I had only imagined her there.

A sharp kick to my middle brought my focus back. The pear-shaped young sailor cut the rope around the Velcro ties on my wrists from the rusting bollard, poked the barrel of his machine gun into my middle and ordered me to my feet. His partner gave me a hand up, then slapped me around to face the ferry's interior and prodded me forward. They marched me into the sheltered expanse, close to the pen where they had the sleepy Sammi incarcerated and signaled me to halt. They took up sentry posts on either side of me and barked something guttural in Russian.

Gorby the Gobbler approached me with a surly stride. "So now you are my guest, Mr. Holman, for a little sea cruise. Don't you just love the fresh salt air?"

"Fresh? It smells like the chemical bath in a photographer's darkroom around here!" I forced a grin behind my words.

The old soldier grinned back. "Unfortunately, you will not be returning to port. I only wish your little Jew pal could be with us, but she will get hers soon, so nothing to worry about. My associates are even now combing the area around Galveston for her. We know she came from Rockport with you to save her precious elephant."

I tried to smile back at him the best I could.

"Maybe it is best that she is not here with us. It will be so much fun to make her watch the video I will be filming as we torture her little elephant child!" The man laughed manically. "And when she has seen her lovely baby elephant destroyed, and her knight in shining armor cut down to a sniveling worm, we will slowly kill her as well! Is this what you wanted Mr. Holman? Because you have brought this all on yourself by interfering in my business. You were warned more than once, but you paid no mind. We could have paid you well to turn your head. We might even have been able to use you in our business!"

I spat in his direction again, earning myself another whack with a rifle butt.

"Yes, Mr. Holman," Gorby hissed, "you may act as manly as you please while you are here as my guest, because in a few hours, you will be the guest of Davy Jones! As soon as we are far enough out into the Gulf, I will be scuttling this old tub of rust, along with you, your little brown helpers and what's left of your silly elephant. But before I send you to the bottom, I will have you watch as I peel the thick skin from your baby elephant one small square at a time. I will enjoy doing this, and even more, I will enjoy filming this on video so that I can show it to your elephant girl as she is raped and tortured!" Again, the man let loose with a sick spasm of laughter, his eyes rolling back into his head and his whole body quivering in sadistic delight.

"As you and your pals slowly become a feast for the sharks, my pilot will be flying me and my men back to Houston where I will have a solid alibi for all this time we are spending at sea. You and your helpers will either drown or be eaten by the sharks that the blood of your precious elephant will attract. Frankly, I could care less which it is... But I will tell your lady the most gruesome story I can invent as I cause her intense physical pain before I kill her!"

With that the man nodded to his minions and one of them delivered a blow to my head with the small machine pistol from his belt, sending me to dreamsville.

CHAPTER THIRTY

I was dreaming that I was sleeping under a waterfall somewhere in Africa or South America. The place in my dream was very much like the Schweitzer Falls on the Disneyland Jungle Cruise ride. I tried to open my eyes, but my eyelids seemed to be glued together. When I finally popped one orb free, I was looking up into Yolanda's beautiful face. She was squeezing a wet rag over my head and, when she saw I was coming around, she held a finger to her lips for silence. I softly crooked "Water. Please."

Yolanda lifted my head and brought a small plastic bottle to my lips, but there wasn't much in it. I drained the warm liquid then fell back to the deck. It was still dark all around us but with a hint of dawn's light showing around the edges, probably close to sunrise. I had no idea of the time. I could feel the vessel pitching about in the rough waters of the Gulf.

Yolanda tore the Velcro ties from my wrists and ankles, dropping them to the deck. "The Russians are drunk," she told me. "Gorby and Chelnikov started drinking vodka after they had you knocked out. They told the two young guards to watch you closely, but as soon as their masters went off to party, the boys found a bottle of their own and crawled off to a corner of the main deck. I cut Payush and Budhan loose and told them to hide down below in the engine room until we call for them."

I rubbed circulation back into my wrists as I looked around us. "So where is everyone else?" I whispered.

"Gorby and Chelnikov are up in the wheelhouse," she told me

in a subdued voice. "The two helpers are out on the open deck. They're probably both passed out by now."

I motioned my head fore and aft and Yolanda turned her own in a nod to the south end of the ferry. I narrowed my eyes where she was looking, saw two lumps snoring near the boat's car loading ramp. An empty bottled rolled to and fro between the two with the ship's rocking. Getting my legs under me, I silently charged, crouched and head down, toward the shadows. At the last minute, I dived at them, hitting the first man hard and knocking him into his sleeping companion. My momentum kept us going. Near the rear lip of the ramp, I put the brakes on and grabbed a rail, but the two men kept rolling right over the edge and into the Gulf's dark green waters.

The first man sank and was pulled under the slowly moving boat's hull, but his companion came alive with a scream. He was shouting something in Russian as he flailed in the waves. Probably some take off on "I can't swim."

I quickly rolled back into the shadows of the boat's starboard railing. Once in the darkest darkness, I dragged myself back below the overhanging deck where Yolanda waited, holding her breath. Budhan's and Payush's heads popped up from a hatchway briefly, but Yolanda signaled them back into hiding.

It took a moment, but we soon heard Gorby shout out to his men. "What's going on down there? What is it?"

His answer was a last loud gurgle from the Gulf as his non-floating henchmen disappeared beneath the waves of our wake.

With wild eyes, Yolanda took my hand and led me to a grimy ladder that spilled toward the ferry's bilges, where we'd seen our two helpers pop up seconds before. Looking over the lip of the engine room hatch, I could see a portly figure slowly and unsteadily navigating the ladder from the upper decks. "Mikhail? Sergei? What's going on down there?"

The man's foot missed a rung, near the bottom of the ladder, and he fell sideways onto the deck, scraping his face on the hard steel decking. Lifting his head with a groan, he came face-to-face with the Velcro ties that Yolanda had taken from my wrists.

"Ahhh!" he roared. "Holman? What have you done, Holman? You know you cannot escape. There is nowhere you can go! I will have your life, and I will make you suffer a long time for this if you have hurt my men!"

"I need some kind of weapon," I whispered to Yolanda. "There must be something. A flare gun? A heavy fire extinguisher?"

Yolanda simply shook her head. And then I saw it, not five feet from the hatch I was peering out of. It was some kind of life preserver gizmo. One of those aluminum poles with a half-moon hook affixed to the end that could be extended over the side to pull a body fallen overboard back to safety. The bolts that held the crescent life ring to the stick didn't look too solid, coated with rust and something else of a greenish cast.

I pulled myself up, leaned as far as I could onto the deck and finally managed to bring the tail end of the stick toward me. The scraping sound brought the fallen man's head slowly up and around, but he couldn't see us in the darkness. Dragging the possible weapon into the hatch where we hid, I took a closer look, then I started twisting the hook back and forth against its moorings. After a dozen repetitions, the bolts snapped and the hook fell away, leaving a jagged edge where the bolts had previously connected to the ring.

"I think I've got a spear," I mumbled to Yolanda.

"Or a javelin," she whispered back. "How's your throwing arm?"

"I don't know about that... Wait a minute!" my brows knitted in thought. "I seem to remember these ass-wipes having some trouble getting Sammi to walk aboard the ship. Chelnikov had a rifle. I remember I was terrified, as I thought he was going to shoot her and be done with it.

"But after he fired what must have been a dart at Sammi, she just kinda slowed down and followed them like she was drunk. A tranquilizer dart! It must have been a tranquilizer dart. A powerful one if it could slow something the size of an elephant! So where is that rifle now?"

"Holman, are you sure of this?"

"I'm sure there was a rifle... But as to where it might be now? It must be on board here somewhere! If we could find that rifle!"

The figure on the deck slowly stood with a roar. It was Gorby the Gobbler and he was pissed. He rushed out onto the deck to find the empty vodka bottle still rolling back and forth but no sentries. The man kicked the bottle into the drink as he called out, "Chelnikov! Chelnikov, wake up you drunken sod! Holman has gotten loose and our guards are gone!"

I checked the point on my crude spear. It wasn't especially sharp, but was probably toxic as hell. "Yo, you need to create a diversion," I told her. "Run down the deck, shout out to them! Anything to grab their attention so I can get to the upper deck to check that helicopter. I flew some helicopters in the Coast Guard. With luck, maybe I can fly this one to get Sammi out of here. And us too!"

"Dave...."

"Just do it!" I hissed as I charged off in the direction away from Gorby.

When I was around a corner behind the stairs and out of sight, I heard Yolanda call out in her finest Brooklyn accent, "Hey, Sailor! Over here! Lookin' for a good time sailor?"

Gorby spun around and focused on her. "You! What are you doing here! Chelnikov, it's the girl! The elephant girl is here on board! Start the helicopter! Now we can sink the ship and kill them all along with their stupid elephant!"

I peered around the corner as he made a lunge toward Yolanda. In fear that he might grab her, I stepped out on deck, lifted my make-shift spear to my shoulder and put everything I had behind it. The pole flew from my hand, arched high across the deck and caught Gorbenko Sergejevič on the side of his neck, pushing him forward to slam his body against the bulkhead near the other set of stairs to the passenger deck. His arms lifted up towards my javelin, waving frantically about but without making purchase on the metal stick dangling from his jugular. His blood poured forth across the deck as his body danced a dance of death.

I turned to find Yolanda behind me, one hand at her throat. In the distance, I heard the engines of the helicopter cough to life. I pressed Yolanda behind me and we backed into the shadows of the car deck. I loudly whispered for our two Indian helpers to get up on deck with us.

Chelnikov advanced cautiously down from the upper decks looking furtively around him. Fortunately, he didn't notice his boss collapsed at the edge of the open deck space. "I'm going to open the sea cocks," he shouted to his superior, although there was no other cohort to hear him. "The motors are warming up. Meet me topside in five minutes and we will leave this place and return to Houston! It is good that this elephant along with our enemies will be well under the ocean by the time we return home!" In his haste, he didn't see our small group huddled in the darkness near Sammi's pen.

When Chelnikov's head was out of sight below the deck, I quickly pulled myself up the ladder to the pilot house and the revving chopper. The old, olive-green bird had some darker patches in the paint on the sides and nose. On closer inspection I could see the faint shadow of Russian red stars covered over with the newer coating of pigment. This helicopter was ex-Russian army, so how did it end up in Texas? Had my captives stolen the aircraft and flown it all the way from Eastern Europe? How could they have gotten it through American defenses? Or had it been brought over to Houston in a container ship? No matter, it was here now and probably our only means of escape.

I climbed into the whirly-bird's cockpit to check the controls and the gauges. All the writing on warning plaques and gauges was in Cyrillic script, but the setup was all pretty standard. Nothing here I couldn't handle. Then the thought struck me. There was no room in an old Sikorsky to rescue an elephant.

I decided to check in the cargo area. Maybe there was a net or something. What I found, behind the pilot's seat, was the tranquilizer dart rifle along with a pouch filled with ammunition. Holman one, Russians nothing! But I was still at a loss for how we would save Sammi if the ferry actually sunk beneath us. Even if the cargo area was larger, how do you get a timid young pachyderm up into an aircraft? I *did* notice a winch and heavy steel cable on an arm that could be swung out from the cargo bay doors.

Slinging the rifle over my left shoulder, I jumped out of the bird and headed back down the ladder to the passenger deck, where I met Yolanda and the boys. I quickly explained our situation. We huddled in the shadows of the large salon brainstorming our predicament. Budhan and Payush decided to set off in search of anything that could be used as a cargo net.

Just after they left, Yolanda and my discussion was interrupted by heavy footsteps coming up the stairs from the car deck. We ducked behind a row of benches. Chelnikov popped up from below and bounded toward the ladder to the top deck. Thinking fast, I loaded a dart and aimed the gun in his direction.

My first shot tore into his thigh and only seemed to anger the man. He hopped around and hollered what must have been obscenities in his native tongue. Yolanda handed me a second dart. In his dance, he turned toward our direction to present a good, full-body target. I sent the second shot deep into his chest.

Chelnikov reared back, started to shout, then did a little more Terpsichore across the wide salon area. Yolanda rushed forward, put an arm around his shoulder and began walking him toward the open area of the deck. Chelnikov smiled, as though he were suddenly entranced with this new lady showing interest in him. My lady walked him to the edge of the deck, gave him a little tap on the back, and our Russian pitched over the side, a grin on his face as though it was he having the last laugh.

CHAPTER THIRTY-ONE

Payush's smiling face appeared at the top of the stairs. "We found some old life rafts," he called out in his sing song voice. "They have a layer of webbing below the bottom canvas to support the weight of passengers, I believe. Perhaps we could rip this out to make a net?"

Yolanda was still staring over the side where Chelnikov had sunk beneath the waves. I called to her, she shook her head quickly to clear her thoughts after pushing a man to his certain death, and we both ran to the hatchway to check what the guys had found.

"We'll have to do something quick," I reminded everyone as I felt the old tub lurch to starboard. "If he's opened up those valves, this rust bucket could be turning turtle within the next fifteen minutes!"

There were two rafts stored in a vertical closet toward the center of the main deck. The ring that provided floatation was old foam packed in canvas, but dampness and rats had torn wide gaps in the heavy cloth covering. The webbing, however, was solid nylon, soiled but intact. I found the spear I tossed into Gorby and used the rough and bloody edge of its point to tear the fabric from the nylon netting. If we spaced it out properly under Sammi's tummy and legs, we might have a chance.

My next job was to get back up to the top deck and further check out the helicopter. I was pretty sure I could fly the son-of-a-bitch, but even if the winch still operated could it lift a half a ton of elephant into the sky and set her safely down again? The sky was turning a rosy pink behind the whirlybird as I reached the boat's roof.

In the bird's cargo bay, I found the lever that operated the cargo lifting apparatus. The arm groaned and fought me as I tried to push it out from the wide doors, but by pulling myself up on the metal bar and swinging my weight out and back, I got it to move slightly, then a little more. I finally let go and gave it a mighty heave which sent it out to its full extension.

I shouted, "Yes," and gave myself a double thumbs-up, then descended from the boat's roof to see how things were coming along below.

Payush had found some heavy coils of rope behind the rafts in the storage area and was weaving the two sets of webbing together while Budhan tied more rope from the outer edges of our make-shift net that could be fastened to the lift's big hook.

"Yo has gone down to talk to Sammi," Payush told me. "Yo must make her very calm and then walk her out to the open deck where we can connect her to the lift cable. Right now Sammi is very frightened and not at all happy!"

The man tugged at his handiwork, then smiled up at me. "The ropes will hold it together. We now have our net! I will go help Yolanda!"

Budhan bundled up the mass of webbing and tilted his head toward the ladder. I led the way, helping the man carry his large bundle up the steep ascent to the pilot house and the top of the ferry. Budhan's large knotted loops slipped easily over the hook on the lift cable.

"The trick," he shouted over the engine's roar and the whoop-whooping of the rotors, "will be to get Sammi to walk onto the net so we can secure it beneath her."

As he said it, the old tub of rust made another hard lurch. She was starting to sink more quickly. I motioned Budhan to step onto the left skid as I strapped myself into the pilot's seat and pushed the stick slowly forward to engage the rotors. The vintage bird bucked a bit, but finally made purchase on a bite of air and lifted haltingly off the ferry about a yard. I moved us forward until we had cleared the main superstructure, then put her into hover mode as Budhan climbed into the bay and began lowering the cable.

Below us, Payush spread the bulk of the descending net out on the deck while Yolanda tickled Sammi under her massive chin and coaxed her forward through the tunnel of ropes to the center of what could be her salvation. When the hesitant pachyderm reached the midpoint, Budhan began tightening the cable. Yolanda climbed up onto Sammi's back and Payush took hold of the ropes. Budhan brought the net as high as he dared, then reached down a hand from the skids to grab Payush by his wrist and pull him up onto the skid before they both crawled into the cargo bay.

Yolanda wove her legs into the netting along Sammi's side and grabbed the overhead supporting ropes with both hands, giving me a thumbs-up with her right hand when she was secure. Beneath her the ferry pitched forward, the old girl's nose rolling to starboard and down into the Gulf's green waters. The ferry slid forward under the waves just as the hot, bright, sun came over the horizon to replace her.

As elephant and girl lifted into the dawn sky Sammi started

trumpeting a happy song. She seemed to like flying. A real live Disney Dumbo!

Budhan came forward and parked his thin form in the co-pilot's seat with a big grin. "Holman, you are the hero! You are the man of steel!"

"We're not home yet," I reminded him, looking glum. Then I turned my head and gave him a smile of my own. "But we're doing pretty well so far. And you and Payush are just as much heroes as I am."

"And please," he beamed, "not to forget Yolanda, the woman who rides an elephant in the sky!"

I flew due north by the old Sikorsky's compass. Soon there was a thin, green line beyond the Plexiglas canopy where sea met sky, and then we began to make out the outline of Galveston Island on the horizon. It didn't seem to be that far away. We reached the shore and a few early dog walkers glanced up from the beach to give surprised looks at this old green bird coming overhead with a girl mounted on an elephant trailing beneath. I kept my eyes open for a clear stretch of sand long enough and wide enough for me to put my cargo down safely.

Finding a good spot I dispatched Payush back out onto the bird's left skid and Budhan to the controls of the winch. We descended slowly until the elephant's feet touched the sand. Then the line went slack so Payush reached down and pulled the ropes from the hook to free Sammi. Yolanda had climbed down from her baby's back and was untangling the ecstatic pachyderm's feet from the old webbing.

I flew clear of the beast and landed about a hundred yards down the beach. Budhan jumped down and ran back to kiss Sammi on the forehead and give Yolanda a big hug. I left the engine idling and went back to check that everyone was okay. Before I reached my cohorts, Sammi made a charge for the water, diving in and swimming around for a short time to emerge trumpeting her joy.

CHAPTER THIRTY-TWO

While on the beach, I managed to raise Hickok on a cell phone borrowed from a pair of amused beach walkers. I arranged with him that I would fly to the FBI's staging area just outside Houston. The agent sounded hesitant at first, then doubtful, but I managed to convince him I *did* have a helicopter that belonged to the Russians and that I could fly it.

He told me that once I was in the air I should backtrack to the ship channel and then follow the water up toward the city. "Just past a large Shell tank farm on the right, you'll see some green buildings surrounded by an asphalt lot. I hate to sound cliché, but even from the air, you could say it screams government compound. I'll have some men out in the lot to guide you down. And I'll put a call in to the FAA to make sure the Air Force doesn't shoot you out of the sky before you get here."

He thought for a moment, then added, "Don't bring the girl, Holman. We'll let you help us out, maybe even come with us to make the bust, but I don't want the girl involved!"

The couple who'd lent me their phone were still sitting at the water's edge fascinated, watching Sammi roll over and over in the shallow surf, so I handed their phone to Yolanda and told her to call Darpaknu to have him bring the truck down to Galveston and pick her and Sammi up. Yolanda took the phone down to where its owners sat to get directions on how Darpaknu could find this particular location on the long, narrow barrier island. Our baby elephant was long overdue at the refuge in Tennessee.

Back in the chopper, I noted that the fuel was now less than one quarter tank. I didn't know just how far I'd have to go to reach the FBI's location, but I'd have to hope it wasn't too far. As long as I could reach the place and touchdown, I could let them worry about refueling it and getting it out of there.

CHAPTER THIRTY-THREE

The task force of police had witnessed the ferry boat's departure after Yolanda had sent the coordinates of the Russian's camp to authorities. She had let the two federal agents know that she would be attempting to rescue me and Sammi. CIA teams, as well as FBI agents had run the location through their computers and done covert surveillance of the area. The government men and local law enforcement were simply waiting for a confirmation that these people presented a clear and present danger.

My return from the sinking ferry gave them the evidence they needed to get a judge's nod and set their operation in motion. By the time I landed the Russian's helicopter in their compound, Hickok and Bishop had assembled a heavily armed SWAT type team to approach the gates of the Russian's property from the road as well as the channel. Aircraft would be standing by as well, helicopters more modern and sophisticated than the old Sikorsky I had used to rescue Sammi and my crew. From the water we had a team of Navy seals in Zodiac boats waiting for the signal to come ashore. I only hoped that Yolanda and her elephant boys were safe on their lonely stretch of Galveston beach.

In the broad and bright daylight of eleven o'clock in the morning, a single figure in cargo shorts and a Hawaiian shirt stood before the gate of what we knew to be the Russian encampment. He rang the buzzer and then shouted, "Hey, is anybody home?"

The man's answer was a burst of automatic weapon fire just over his head, although he wore heavy body armor over his chest for personal protection. The Hawaiian-shirted figure tossed a grenade over the gate before he dropped to the ground. The fact that someone had fired on a federal agent bearing a warrant and acting under orders gave the rest of the troop license and a good excuse to advance on the premises.

Seals swarmed up from the oily channel as a pair of paratroopers came down from the skies. An armored vehicle driven by Hickok, carrying Bishop, myself and a handful of Harris and Aransas County deputies in the rear rolled over the razor wire fence leveled by the grenade and into the fenced field.

The dozen men that poured forth from the old tin Quonset hut on the property didn't know what to do. Half of them came out shooting while others ran forth waving white handkerchief banners or with bare hands in the air.

As their leaders, Gorby and Chelnikov, were nowhere to be found, many of the men were fearful of what might become of them. The rabble assembled outside of the buildings were quickly subdued. The FBI team and I were able to enter the old Quonset hut that the Russians had stood so eager to defend.

In spite of what we'd suspected, we were not ready for the sight that awaited us. Along the walls were stacked filthy old mattresses. Once pretty young girls languished on these pads, now hollow eyed with souls devoid of hope. Each station was positioned under a beam supporting shackles, which secured these young girls to their bunks. The scent of depression hung heavy in the air. The posture of many of the young ladies' told us that they were already dead in their hearts. All hope of life had been lost. They had surrendered to being pieces of meat, ready to be used by whomever.

Behind us, men in camouflage uniforms stormed the room. One by one, the young girls were set free. At first, they couldn't comprehend the kindness that was being offered them, but as the soldiers helped them to their feet and offered blankets to cover their nakedness, they began to come around. Some actually smiled and one gave her liberator a strong hug and a chaste kiss.

Deputy Carlson, in his Aransas County uniform, met the girls as they were led outside and helped guide them to a Harris County Sheriff's Department bus. A small dark-haired girl gave him a double-take, then stopped in front of him.

"Sam!" she exclaimed. "Did Mikey tell you I'd been kidnapped? Oh God it's good to see you. I didn't think I'd ever see a friendly face again."

Carlson smiled at her. "I asked to be part of this investigation when Cousin Mikey told me you had been kidnapped. I told your parents I wouldn't rest until you were back and safe at home."

The girl looked down at her feet, then raised her head to look Sam Carlson in the eye. "Thank you, Sam!" Then she burst into tears. Her "Thank you from all of us" was followed by a loud sniffle. "Mikey said he thought you were crazy joining the cops... but I'm so glad that you did!"

CHAPTER THIRTY-FOUR

T here was just one missing piece to the puzzle. Someone was still pulling strings here, someone that stood outside our dragnet. The men who were captured knew very little of the hierarchy above them. They knew only that they did as they were told, just as they had for many years in the old country, without question. Only one man, some kind of senior sergeant among the ranks, was willing to speculate on the name of a big man above and beyond Gorby and Chelnikov, a man that was little more than a shadowy legend.

He had met Demetri Lubikov only one time. This was the name he gave us and the man came up on the CIA's computers after a lengthy search. Orders were quickly issued and the old senior Russian officer was captured by Harris County deputies at Houston's older Hobby Airport as he boarded a Southwest Airlines flight for Orlando, Florida. He had in his overnight bag a second passport in the name of Paul James Smith bearing his photograph along with a ticket in this new alias for Riyadh, Saudi Arabia.

Demetri Lubikov, alias Paul James Smith, suddenly became a very popular man. Law enforcement agencies from Miami, Florida, to northern Mexico, all at once wanted a piece of him. Thanks to my work, first for Lupe Martinez and later following the farther trail of missing girls, Aransas County got the first crack at him. The FBI had him brought to the Rockport Detention Center, where the guard on him was tripled to include locals, feds and Texas Rangers. There was no question that the man and his little crime syndicate was guilty of crimes on an international scale that touched five U.S. states and much of northern Mexico.

By the next morning, officers from Interpol arrived from Europe with more pieces to contribute to the puzzle. Our man Lubikov was the link to syndicates in Japan, China and the Arab world that supplied young girls, for sale or rent, to anyone wealthy enough to pay the big bucks.

Jean Valin, the lead detective from the Brussels team, told me that life expectancy for these girls was not good. A few became real companions to the men that bought them, but most were tossed away like trash after they were used.

"Although men pay thousands of dollars for them," Jean said, "they are regarded as less then yesterday's cold scrambled eggs once they've provided their brief pleasures!"

Someone must have repeated this to Lupe Martinez. When I left the police station, she came up to me in tears of rage, demanding that I try to kill the man if I got a chance. "I'll keep paying you for the rest of your life if you can do this! I'll support you forever, Holman, I'll do anything for you!"

I tried hard to keep a serious face as I explained the facts to her. "If I did something like that, my career, and maybe even my life would be over. You're better off letting the system handle him."

Then I gave her my highest point of comfort. "Lupe, we are lucky that we caught this man here in Texas and that Texas has the first shot at him. If he'd made it out of the country, most of Europe no longer has the death penalty. While other countries may find him guilty and lock him up for life, we are going to fight to keep him here in Texas where the state will see to it that he dies by a lethal injection."

She smiled through her tears and put her arms around me to give me a hug. Over her shoulder, I could see Yolanda's gray Thing turning onto Cornwall from Magnolia Street. Chandra was riding shotgun and two of her friends were seated in the back. Chandra vaulted over the Volkswagen's short door and ran over to throw one arm around her mother and one around me, joining in our hug.

"I think you've done well," Yolanda told me when the other ladies let me go as she moved in to put her own arms around me. She laid a big kiss on me, pulled her face back to look into my eyes and said, "Thanks for saving me as well!"

Then she held onto me even tighter. Her next kiss was pretty steamy hot and lasted almost a full minute. "And thanks for saving Sammi! I just got a call from Budhan and the boys that Sammi's arrived at the preserve. My rescue mission accomplished as well. I love you, Dave Holman!"

EPILOGUE

Things went quickly once all the players were rounded up. By now our Russians were well on their way through the Federal justice system with interested parties from other countries keeping tabs. It looked as though at least Demetri Lubikov would take his place on death row over the protests of the European nations involved. The other young men would be spending a big chunk of their lives behind bars as guests of the United States criminal justice system.

As I was reading all about it in the Corpus Christi paper, there was a timid knock on my door. Yolanda stood and went to answer it. Buster Burreson, in clean cargo shorts and his finest Reyn Spooner Hawaiian shirt, was standing on our doorstep.

"Remember me?" he inquired.

"Daughter named Amy who was a friend of Chandra? I remember you." I stood and extended my hand. "I was just reading about the case in the paper."

"You did us all a great service, Mr. Holman. I mean all of us parents with young, vulnerable daughters. I don't know what I would have done if someone grabbed our Amy."

"That's good to hear, Mr. Burreson..."

"Please, call me Buster! I'd like to think that we're friends."

"Ah, of course, Buster. But as I was about to say, I was just doing my job, both as a detective and as a concerned citizen."

Buster Burreson turned to Yolanda. "This man is just too modest!" he smiled at her. "Anyway, I wanted to invite you to a little party the wife, Amy, and I are throwing. It's for all those girls that you helped to rescue."

I raised my eyebrows. "A party for the girls? They had a pretty rough experience. Are you sure they're ready for a party?"

"Oh, most definitely, ah, Dave, sure they went through a lot, they went through a sort of hell. But they were all there together. They supported each other the best they could… And they formed quite a bond by what they all experienced. They're like a family now, like sisters, even Chandra, although she wasn't there with them for very long.

"It's going to be in the Rockport-Fulton High School Performing Arts center. Our Amy will be the official hostess. We've hired a local rock band and we're having the affair catered by that lady chef who used to have the Mermaids restaurant out on Highway 35 just south of Market Street."

"I'm impressed! This is really thoughtful of you, Buster!"

"I'm also bringing in a lady from Austin who does glamour make-over's." he told us. "She'll spend time with each girl individually to help rebuild their self-esteem by showing them what makeup best brings out their features. I want each one of them to know just how beautiful she really is, and how unique and special. I want them each to realize their own worth Mr. Ho… Dave!"

"Thank you, Buster!" Yolanda added. "This is all such a great idea! I know how easy it is for teenagers to feel bad about themselves, especially after the trauma of being turned into faceless captives."

"So will you both join us?" Buster asked. "It will be this Saturday evening, from around six o'clock. I know many of the girls would like the opportunity to thank you personally!"

I Looked at Yolanda, who was beaming down at me in my chair. "How could we refuse? It will be a great honor," she answered for both of us.

"Will Detective Sanchez be joining us?" I asked.

"Of course," Buster grinned. "And the girls have also told me I must invite a deputy sheriff named Sam. Would you know this man? Or where I can contact him?"

Yolanda let loose with a giggle, so I jumped in. "Sam Carlson is a young officer with the Aransas County Sheriff's Office. One of the rescued girls knows him through a cousin of his in Corpus. I'll make sure he gets an invitation."

"And, you had better make sure he has Saturday off," Yolanda added, then she gave a thoughtful pose. "Better yet, this should be an *official* duty for him, Dave. You tell the sheriff to have him there in full dress uniform and looking his impressive best!"

Who am I to argue with a lady?

ABOUT THE AUTHOR

Skoot Larson is a native Los Angelino, a musician, music critic and a Viet Nam veteran. He has also worked as a disc jockey, actor, speech therapist, stand-up comedian, behavioral counselor and streetcar conductor. His previous works include the Lars Lindstrom Zen-Jazz Mystery series, a black-humor novel about health care in America entitled "Apollo Issue," and a political humor novel, "The Palestine Solution." Skoot lives with his two cats in Rockport, Texas.

www.ingramcontent.com/pod-product-compliance
Lightning Source LLC
Chambersburg PA
CBHW070045260626
47159CB00005B/2128